The Many Secrets My Husband Kept

Loryn Landon

Chapter One

Justin

"You like how I give this big dick to you, don't you?!" I rhetorically asked.

"Hell yeah! Harder! Is that all you got?"

Pounding and thrusting crazy as we met each other stroke for stroke our bodies were one. We were in sync as our bodies left us both in the most euphoric feeling that only WE could give to each other.

Switching positions from being the giver to now becoming the receiver, my lover whose face was covered but I knew all so well, started giving me all that they had.

"Ouuu that's my spot, damn it! Harder, right there! Harder I said!"

Both of us, yelling out explicit language, moaning, groaning, and panting heavily as we continued to ram our bodies against each other. It was, by far, THE best feeling that I had ever felt.

Just as I was reaching my peak... I woke up.

Even though it was my day off, my body was accustomed to waking up super early every morning. That and the fact the dream I just had had me waking up at 4am with a morning woody ready to bust. Getting up to use the washroom in hopes of releasing some of the pressure in my protruding dick, I tried not to make too much noise. I didn't want to wake up my wife, who was lying in the bed beside me, just yet. Making it back to the bed and getting in quietly, I couldn't help but to notice her juicy, phat ass peeking from under the nightgown that she had on. My wife, Ava was a very sexy woman. She was any man's dream girl. I lucked up when she and I got together and scored once she fell in love with me. Having her on my arm gave me the boost of confidence that I needed every day that let me know that I was still THE man. Today was her first day back at work. She didn't need to be up for another hour, plenty of time for us to get it in.

Scooting closer to her so were in the spooning position, I ran one of my hands slowly up her smooth, carmel thigh stopping just as I got to her core. Since she didn't have any panties on, I had easy access to her sweet budding flower. Taking my forefinger and sticking it in my mouth, I covered it with saliva then slide it between her legs into her phat, juicy cat.

"Mmmmm, babe," she moaned as she spread her legs open, allowing me to have more access.

"Let me taste that cat, baby girl." I whispered in her ear.

Turning and lying on her back, she assumed the position. Crawling between her legs I started feasting on her juicy pussy. I loved to eat her out. I actually preferred to eat her out over having sex with her. I know that sounds crazy, but between having sex and oral with my wife, I preferred oral. It wasn't that sex with her wasn't good. It was very good to say the least. I just loved to go down on her. The sexual position that I loved the most was back door action, pussy fucking didn't completely satisfy me. I just never let my wife know that because I didn't want her to feel any type of way about it.

Ava, however, loved to have sex. She really didn't care what position we fucked in, although her favorite position was either riding my wood or doggie style. She loved it when I hit it from the back and after much convincing she grew to love having anal sex as well. Whenever I was feeling super horny and really needed to get one off, I'd initiate doggie style so I could go from her cat to her ass with easy access. Hands down the best!

"Ahhh Justin, baby that feels so good," Ava moaned as I slurped, licked and sucked on her clit and pussy lips.

"Mmmmmmm," I hummed as I locked my lips on her clit.

"Ouuu! Ouuu! I'm about to cum J," she moaned out as she rocked her hips against my face, grabbing the top of my head while holding it in place. "Don't stop, right there baby."

Stopping was the last thing that was on my mind. I could feel her body tensing up as I wrapped my arms around her waist making sure to lock her in her place. I could tell from how tense she was and how she was trying to back up that she was about to have an intense orgasm. Flicking my tongue on her clit as I continued to slurp on it, a move I knew she loved for me to do, brought her to her peak. Feeling, as well as tasting, a gush of her juices as she squirted in my mouth had instantly put my dick on swole mode. My shit was so hard it started to hurt. I needed to get it wet... asap!

"Turn that ass around. Let me hit that shit from the back!" I demanded once I felt her pussy had stopped thumping against my lips.

Doing as I had instructed, she got in the perfect doggie style position; face down ass up with a perfect arch in her back. Slapping her on one of her juicy cheeks, watching it as her shit jiggled, I hurriedly got into formation behind her. Sliding my 9 ½ inch wood deep into the folds of her wet pussy, I had to contain myself from not busting too soon. Grabbing her ass cheeks, holding one of her cheeks open so that I could slide my finger in her tight ass, I had to get her exit hole ready for my grand entrance.

"Sssssss ahhh, J," Ava moaned as she threw her phat ass back at me as I thrusted in and out of her wet pussy while playing with her anal opening.

Ava enjoyed anal, but I had to make sure that she was super horny to be down for it. That was why I made it a point to give her some good head before we got started. Ava was a closet freak. For some reason, she always tried to be more modest than she really was. I didn't know if it was because she thought I would judge her or what. But when she was really in the mood, she enjoyed anal just as much as I did.

"Relax baby. I need to feel that phat ass." I groaned. Sliding the tip of my thick mushroom head out of her wet pussy slowly, invading the opening of her ass and not stopping until I was balls deep in then I went to work. The shit felt so good, as the tight walls of her ass hugged my shaft just the way I liked.

Feeling nothing but pure bliss, I went in, fucking her in the ass, rubbing on her clit and finger fucking her pussy. My Johnson continued to invade the walls of her ass, as the sensations running through my body had me damn near weak in the knees. All you could hear throughout the room were the two of us moaning and groaning, her ass cheeks smacking against my thighs as I gave her some hardcore work.

Feeling pressure in my dick as I felt my cum rising to the top, I started to go faster... harder. I was beating that ass up, giving her all that I had.

"Ahhh baby, fuck! You about to make me cum," Ava all but sang out. I stayed in rhythm, grunting and moaning, trying my hardest to contain my composure. I wanted to scream out like a bitch... the shit had me gone!

"FUCK!! I'm cumming too! Got damn it!" I bellowed as I released my load deep in the walls of her ass.

Looking down all I could see were my cum juices dripping from the small crevices between her asshole and my dick that was still halfway inside of her. Ava clearly busted a hard one too because her juices were dripping from her core. What a sexy view!

"Fuck girl, that morning sex be the best sex. I swear it is!" I gloated, breathing heavy as I slid my dick out of her ass then headed to the bathroom to shower.

"Whew! Tell me about it. That was good babe."

"Thanks sweet stuff. I wanted to give you a little something special on your first day back at work. I had to make sure to give you and all that ass something to think about throughout your day."

"You so silly, but I love it." Ava giggled as she stepped into the shower behind me.

Taking turns washing each other off, I started with her then we switched positions and she washed me off. Our shower was big enough for three people. It had a bench built into it on one side that was EVERYTHING when it came to fucking in the shower. Once Ava was done washing me off, she took my dick into her hands and started stroking the tip just the way I liked as she kissed my lips.

"Now let me give you a little something to think about throughout your day," she hissed as I gave into the feelings of pleasure she was giving me.

Dropping to her knees then taking my hard dick into her mouth, she went to work doing what I enjoyed; topping me off. Backing up then lifting one of my legs up onto the shower bench gave her easier access to my balls. As she started tea bagging my shit, I couldn't resist closing my eyes thinking about my lover. All I could think about was if it were my lover instead of Ava topping me off. Ava was a beast at the mouth work she'd give, but she was no match to my lover.

I couldn't help but to think the climax that was building would have been way more intense with my lover, but I wasn't knocking what she was serving. Ava was great at sucking me off, but my lover... whew! My lover did it best and knew exactly what to do to get me to the most intense climax every time. All I could think was that I couldn't wait for Ava to leave, so that I could go and get taken care of the way I liked.

After busting down Ava's throat, we rinsed off then I headed into the bedroom to get dressed.

"So what do you have planned for today?" Ava asked, walking into the bedroom so that she could get dressed for work. "You have the whole day to yourself now that I'm back at work."

"Yep, I do and I'm going to miss you."

"Awww babe, I'm going to miss you too."

"I just have a few errands to run. And I might stop by the gym to get a lil workout in."

"Was our lil workout this morning not enough for you?" Ava giggled.

"It was all good but you know I have to keep this body right and tight. I don't want you leaving me for no young nigga."

"Oh stop it J. You know you're the only man for me."

I finished getting dressed first, so I headed to the kitchen to start a pot of coffee as I did every morning. As I waited for the coffee to brew, I grabbed my phone to see if I had any notifications that needed tending too. The first notification I saw was from my lover. We must have been thinking about each other since it had been a lil minute since we last saw one another.

S.B: I hope we're still on for today? I'm overdue

Me: Me too! Yeah we on. See you soon

S.B: I'll be waiting

I was deep into my text conversation when Ava walked into the kitchen causing me to jump a little. I almost dropped my cellphone. The last thing I needed was for her to catch me texting my dip.

"Smells so good in here! Thanks for making coffee babe." Ava gleamed as she reached into the cabinet, grabbing her to-go coffee tumbler.

Doctoring her coffee up with sugar and cream with a smile on her face as she hummed an unfamiliar tune. Then she put the lid on her cup, grabbed her briefcase, purse and keys then headed for the garage.

"Have a good first day back at work sweetie. I hope those kids don't drive you crazy." I chuckled.

"Thanks babe. I missed my babies, I can't wait to get the day started," Ava replied, kissing me on the lips.

I stood at the garage door as I watched her get into her all-black Kia Telluride. As soon as she backed out of the garage, I closed the garage door ready to get my day started.

My wife worked as a guidance counselor at the high school a few blocks away from where we lived. She loved her job and God bless her for that. She was the only person that I knew that got excited about having to spend the whole day in a building with hundreds of teenagers. Better her than me. I really wasn't a people person like that so being a firefighter was the perfect career choice for me. I'd rather fight fires any day of the week then to have to deal with a bunch of teenagers for a whole day real talk.

I fixed myself a cup of coffee then headed upstairs to put on some cologne and my sneakers so that I could head over to my lover's house. I couldn't wait to get there. This lover was a "new lover" in a way. I was actually cheating on Ava with two people. One person that I had been sleeping with prior to Ava and I dating, and another person I just started fucking fairly recent. We had only been seeing each other for a little over a month.

Ava and I had been together for over two years and two weeks ago we took our relationship to the next level and got married. We went on our honeymoon to Jamaica the day after we got married and spent a week and a half away. We had just returned home this past Thursday and spent every day since we got back together, not giving me any time to dip off. The fact that today I was going to be spending the majority of the day with my dip had me feeling extra excited. It worked out perfectly because I had the day off, I wasn't returning back to work until tomorrow and most importantly, Ava was back to work.

Finishing my coffee gave me the extra pep in my step that I needed to move a little faster than I was. Hitting my neckline and chest with some Diesel cologne, I had to make sure I smelled extra good. I grabbed my wallet, cellphone and keys then headed to garage. I couldn't get to see my lover fast enough as I backed out of the garage and sped down the street.

Ava

Feeling Justin grinding against me trying to pry my legs open caused me to get up a little earlier than I was anticipating, but I was cool with it. Waking up to some of the best head and morning sex was one of the many benefits to becoming Mrs. Justin Miller. We were fresh off of our honeymoon and with as much sex as we had been having, one would think that I was tired of it, but not me. I couldn't get enough of my husband. I loved when our bodies connected, the pleasure that it gave me was nothing but pure satisfaction.

Heading out the house to start my first day back at work was bittersweet. I wanted to stay home with Justin being that he had the day off and wouldn't be returning to work until tomorrow. Since Justin was a firefighter, he had to work 48-hours on and 24-hours off, which meant that I would only get to see him tonight then I'd have to go two whole days without him. I hated that about his job but it was what it was. I had gotten somewhat used to his schedule over the years we dated. I just didn't care for it. I guess I had gotten used to being with him every day all day since we had been spending so much time together since the wedding.

On my drive into work, I decided to call my sister Dawn. I knew that she would be up and starting her day. Her salon was the only hair salon that was open on Mondays in the town that we lived in. My sister was THE best hair stylist around and because of that, her schedule stayed booked. She was the only person that I would allow to do my hair 'cause she was a beast at it. She could style both long and short hair, which was rare in a stylist.

"Hey sissy, I knew I would be hearing from you this morning." Dawn giggled.

It was normal for me to call her every morning on my way to work. Since I had been off and honeymooning, my morning calls to her had been put on hold.

"Hey sissy! I miss our morning talks."

"Me too girly," Dawn gushed then continued. "Girl, I'm trying to rush to get to the shop, but I done ran into some traffic. My client gone be pissed."

"I swear you never on time for shit. I don't understand why you book early appointments when you know you can't get to work on time."

"Shit it don't matter what time I schedule my first appointment for, I always manage to run late."

"That's some crazy shit."

"I know, it's safe to say time is my enemy." Dawn laughed. "So tell me, how does it feel being a married woman now?"

"It feels absolutely amazing sissy. Justin is truly the love of my life. He makes me so happy. I'm so blessed to have him in my life."

"I'm so happy for you sissy. The wedding was absolutely beautiful. You two make a very good looking couple. There for a minute I was worried about you two."

"Thanks sissy that means a lot. I know how you are about the guys I date, so you liking Justin really means the world to me."

"I like him because he is making you happy now. If you like it, I love it... you know how I roll. I just hope he doesn't switch up 'cause he was acting real suspect before the wedding."

"I feel you and I hope he doesn't change up either. I think he was getting a case of cold feet before the wedding honestly. Hell, I would be lying if I said I wasn't nervous about getting married also."

"I'm not talking about before the wedding sissy. I'm talking before the proposal."

"No relationship is perfect Dawn. Yeah, we had a few bumps in the road, but he has been doing a lot better," I defended.

The only thing I hated about discussing my relationship woes with Dawn was the fact that she never allowed for me to forget them. She was the only person, other than my best friend Shane, that I trusted to vent to about my relationship. Before Justin proposed to me, we had gone through what I called a phase. Our relationship had hit rocky times and Justin was spending the majority of his time off with his homeboys instead of me. I was feeling very lonely, ready to end things with him.

When I addressed my feelings with him, he sincerely apologized, claiming that I meant the world to him and wanted to fight for our relationship. Months later, he proposed. I get my sister being concerned, but he and I had been doing just fine so that was what I was going to focus on.

"For now, but you know what people say. After the wedding, folks tend to get super comfortable and start slacking. He already has slacker tendencies, so all I'm saying is I hope he stays on the right path is all."

"I know and I hear you loud and clear. I'm not trying to focus on anything negative. No one is perfect and like I said, ever since I brought my concerns to him there hasn't been an issue since. Now that we are married, things are better than ever, so why focus on the past?"

"Okkkaaayyy! Don't be getting snappy with me ma'am. I'm just looking out for my lil sissy. I want nothing but the best for you and Justin both. Trust and believe that. I just don't like to see or hear you upset is all."

"I get it D and I appreciate you for always being here for me to vent to, but you have to ease up a little. Just try to give Justin a chance. Let's move forward and keep the past woes in the past."

"I get it. All is forgiven just not forgotten. It's hard for me to forget how upset you were when you guys were on the brink of breaking up. I'm glad that he saw your worth and stepped it up. Cause I was seconds away from putting my foot in his ass." Dawn laughed then continued. "You deserve nothing but the best sissy. We have gone through so much with losing mom and dad. A failed relationship is the last thing I want for you or for you to not be happy."

"I get it and that's why I love you to death. Well, I'm pulling up to the school now. I'll talk to you later. Have a good day sissy."

"Love you too. Same to you."

Hanging up with Dawn, I couldn't do anything but shake my head. I knew that she meant well, but sometimes she drove me bonkers bringing up negative vibes. I get why she was so concerned though because when Justin and I were having our issues, I was devastated thinking that he was cheating on me. But every time I'd follow him or check his phone, which he didn't appreciate so he put a password on it, he'd be right where he said he was; with his friends.

Before he and I moved in together, I didn't realize how much time he spent with his friends, but once I moved in, it had become way too much. I was feeling neglected all the time, so as a result, I vented and cried to Dawn just about every day. So I could definitely understand why she was being so guarded and concerned about me. She was only doing what big sisters did.

After parking, I grabbed my things and headed inside the high school to get started with my first day back. Making my way through the crowd of teenagers and approaching the front entrance, I saw Kevin, one of the security guards.

"Welcome back Ms. Smith. It's good to see you," Kevin said as he held the door open for me.

"Thanks Kevin, but it's Mrs. Miller now. It's good seeing you as well."

"Oh snap! Congrats! I didn't know."

"I got married two weeks ago."

"Well, I must say, your husband is a very lucky man."

"Thanks Kevin, I appreciate the compliment. Have yourself a good day," I responded, walking past him then heading to the front office to check in.

Kevin was one of the security guards that had worked at the high school for about as long as I had. He always made it a point to speak to me and occasionally, we would have lunch together in the teacher's lounge. Things between him and I were strictly platonic, although there was an underlying secret that we both were attracted to one another. He was a very handsome man, built similar to Justin. They both were athletes in school, and you could tell that just like with Justin, Kevin frequented the gym to workout often.

Whenever we would chit chat, it would never be about anything serious. We never talked about anything personal. I didn't know his relationship status and he didn't know much about mine. All I knew was that he wasn't married. He never missed an opportunity to compliment me, but that was just how things were between us; playful banter but never crossing any lines. In a small way, I enjoyed it because whenever I was feeling any self-doubt his compliments always reminded me that I still had it, especially when Justin had me feeling not very desirable.

After checking in, I made my way to my office. I decided to send Justin a text just to check in with him. I was still feeling the after-effects of our lovemaking session between my legs and just as he wanted, he sent me on my way with thoughts of him running through my head.

Me: Hey baby, just thinking about u. (heart emoji) Getting ready to start my day. I can't wait to see u when I get home. (kissy face emoji)

Logging into the computer system, for it to be the first day back I was swamped with emails to go through, so I jumped right in. There was an assembly going on to kick off the first day back that started the period before the lunch periods began. By the time I had finished going through my emails and finishing up some paperwork that I needed to work on, it was time for the assembly to start. Checking my phone, I noticed that Justin hadn't texted me back. Remembering that he said he was planning to run errands and go to the gym, I figured he must have been working out and didn't have his phone on him.

Logging off the computer, I headed to the auditorium to get this new school year started. Once the assembly was over, I went straight to the teacher's lounge to eat lunch. I was starving and hadn't eaten all day. There were a couple of other teacher's in the lounge also. Thankfully, it wasn't too crowded so that I could sit at a table by myself. Grabbing my cellphone, I called my bestie Shane to check in with him. I didn't want people in my business because sometimes me and Shane's conversations were filled with all sorts of juicy gossip. I hadn't talked to my homie since the wedding day and I was missing him badly. There was no telling where our conversation would go, because Shane was always up to something. I couldn't wait to catch up with him.

Calling his phone, it went straight to voicemail. Shane was a barber and didn't work on Mondays, so I was surprised that he didn't answer my phone call. Especially since he and I hadn't had a chance to talk much. I figured he must had been on the other line or something. Knowing him he was probably boo'd up. I gave him a few minutes to see if he would call back. When he didn't, I decided to send him a text message.

Me: Hey bestie, I was hoping to catch up with you on my lunch break. You must be boo'd up!! LOL! Miss u! Talk to u later.

Seeing that I had twenty minutes left on my break, I went to the Kindle app on my cellphone and pulled up *The Queen V* by Dr. Jackie from the reality show *Married to Medicine*. I started on this book before the wedding and was only halfway through it. Thus far, it was pretty informative. She touches on all those uncomfortable questions that most women are too nervous or prude to ask their doctors when it comes to vaginal health. Since I hadn't had much time to get any reading done while I was off, I figured I'd read a couple of chapters before heading back to my office.

The second half of my day flew by and I was thankful for that. Today was a pretty easy going day. Tomorrow my day was packed with sessions with the students from my roster. Making my way out the building and to my car, I couldn't get home fast enough. Justin had never replied to my text message that I sent to him earlier. I figured he must have been very busy. I couldn't wait to get home to hear all about how his day went and to spend the rest of my evening boo'd up with my husband.

On the way home, I decided to give Shane another call, in hopes that he was available. I figured my sister was probably busy working on one of her clients and I didn't want to distract her. Plus, I didn't like talking to her while she was doing hair because I didn't like for her clients to be privy to all of our conversations. Thankfully, this time, Shane answered the phone.

Chapter Two

Shane

"Hey baa-booski boo! How was your first day back to work?" I screeched then put my phone on mute to kiss my boo one last time before he walked out the door to leave.

"Hey bestie, wit yo crazy self!" Ava chuckled. "It was grrrreeeeeat! I can't wait to tell you all about it."

"Ouuuu bitch, I can't wait to hear about it. I want all the juicy deets too. Don't leave not a thang out!"

"I called you on my lunch break, but you didn't answer."

"Girl I had some company over. You know today is my day off," I replied with a little disappointment. I truly did want to hear how things went on her honeymoon and hated that I had missed her call.

"I should have known that's why you didn't answer." Ava chuckled. "I called you 'cause I knew it was your day off." Ava giggled. "I feel like it's been forever since we talked."

"It has been forever, boo. We haven't chatted since your wedding."

"That's true."

"So, how was your honeymoon?"

"It was amazing bestie. We spent the majority of the time in our room of course."

"Ouuuuu, y'all so nasty!" I cackled.

"I truly had a great time. I'll have to give you all the 'juicy deets' as you say, when we hook up. So, other than being a playa playa with all your many boos, what's been going on with you?"

"I wouldn't say I'ma playa playa, savage is a better term." I chuckled, causing Ava to laugh. "Me and all my boos have an understanding. They not my only one just like I'm not their only one."

"Lawdy, lawdy friend, I don't know what I'm going to do with you. You know you too much!"

"I'm just saying." I chuckled but was dead ass serious. "Aside from working, I ain't been doing much of nothing just the usual."

"We need to get together soon. Justin has to work tomorrow and this weekend, well Friday and Saturday. So, if you don't have anything planned you should come over. I'll cook and make up some Sangria or something. I was watching Tasty's and saw a recipe for Sangria I wanna try."

"Ouuu that does sound fun, friend. But I don't know about the Sangria though. You always using me as your Guinea pig and shit with dem recipe videos yo ass be watching."

"Don't front Shane, you know those recipes be hittin'."

"Uht friend…"

"Okay, I'll admit, I have messed up a couple of recipes. But for the most part be honest, I have come up with some good ass dishes."

"I'll give you that. You have created SOME fire ass dishes. But baby!!!! Some of those recipes were epic fails chile." I laughed joking with her. She did fuck up a few dishes though, but we always joked with each other like that. "You know Fridays and Saturdays are my busiest days but, for you I can definitely work that into my schedule. Maybe I'll spend the night Saturday, but I'll let you know for sure."

"That sounds good. Welp, I'm pulling up to the house, so I'll chat with you later. Love you, bestie."

"Love you too girl."

As soon as I hung up the phone with Ava, I headed straight for the shower. When she called me earlier, I was face down ass up getting the workout of my entire life. All I wanted to do now was jump in the shower and find something to eat. I hadn't eaten anything since last night, so I was starvin'!

Finishing up in the shower, I headed to my bedroom to find something to wear. I didn't have any plans on going anywhere, plus I was tired from earlier, so I decided to put on some Tommy lounging pants with the tank to match. Figuring I wasn't up to cook anything, I decided to order something from Chiptole on Grubhub. As I waited for my food, I fixed myself a Moscow Mule then went into the den to wait for my food to arrive.

Taking a few sips from my drink, I was feeling relaxed, just the mood I was going for.

Turning on the TV, I went to Netflix to finish watching Ozark. I only had two episodes left and I was anxious as hell to see what was going to happen next. Just as I was getting deep into my show, my cellphone dinged with a notification. Hoping that it was my Grubhub driver I got excited but seeing that it was one of my boos, Dexter texting me, I rolled my eyes then opened the message to see what he wanted.

Dex: You straight

That was code for can I come over.

Me: Not tonight... maybe tomorrow after work

Dex: WYD

Me: Chillin'

Dex: You good

I was fine. I was just exhausted from earlier. I really wasn't up for anymore company.

Me: Yeah... hbu?

Dex: Would be better if I could slid through. You sound like you not wit it though? What's good?

Ugh! I really wasn't up for any more entertaining, but I didn't want to come across as acting funny with him. Dexter and I had been seeing each other on the down low for a little over three years now. We were on the DL because he was keeping the fact that he loved to fuck on men a secret. He had a woman and claimed he was bi-sexual to me, yet he didn't want anyone to know; weak, but very common. Being a gay, black man it seemed like all I could attract were dudes on the DL. In a way, I was fine with it because I wasn't trying to be exclusive to just one person, so being in secret relationships or fuckships as I liked to call them, worked out perfect for me.

The only person that knew about the many guys I secretly fucked on was my bestie Ava. Well, she knew about some of them and she knew "of" the ones that I promised to keep their identities top secret. I didn't tell her about ALL of them because some things were best kept to myself. Unlike the men that I saw, I was 100% gay. I had no desire to ever sleep with a woman, EVER! Ava would always say that I reminded her of Jonathan Fernandez from *Love & Hip Hop New York*. He was a bit more flamboyant than I was in my opinion, but for the most part I could see why she felt that way.

Part of it had to do with my looks. Jonathan and I did look a lot alike and in some ways, I guess one could say that we acted alike, a little. I just wasn't as messy as he was and I dressed way better and was way sexier than he was. I didn't wear flashy clothes. I dressed very metro. Makeup was never and would never be my thing. I was more reserved and chill unless I was forced to be messy. Now if pushed, I could be a force to reckon with.

So back to Dexter, he was like a suga daddy to me. We were around the same age, so I guess that would have made him a young suga daddy. Dexter's pockets were fat and his dick size matched his pockets so for me, fucking with him was a no brainer. He was a hustler and very proud of it. He loved to floss and didn't mind spending money and making sure my pockets stayed fat. So even though I really wasn't up for anymore company today, I didn't want to be shady toward him.

Me: What time you talkin' about coming by?

Dex: Shit soon. I have a quick drop to make then I'll be on my way

Me: OK great. See you then

Putting my show on pause, I headed to my bedroom in a huff to clean up from my earlier romp in the sheets. I usually didn't make it a habit to see two men in the same day, but when you fucked around with people on the DL it was like I had to be available whenever they had the time to get away. I guess that was how side chicks felt when it came time to spend time with the men that belonged to other women. Making it to my room, I changed the sheets on my bed then went back to the den hoping to finish watch Ozark while I waited on my food and for Dexter to arrive.

Just as I was halfway through the last episode, my phone dinged with a notification from Grubhub. About damn time! I was irritated that I had to put my show on pause again, but excited that my food was finally here. The delivery person sent me a text letting me know that they had pulled up and was waiting for me to come outside to get my food.

Making my way outside, I couldn't move fast enough. I got my food and just as the delivery driver was leaving, Dexter pulled up.

I stood there while he parked and waited for him to walk up my driveway so that we could walk into the house together.

"Who just left?"

"What was that?" I asked because I know he saw the big ass brown bag of food in my hand.

"Who that dude was that just left?"

"Ugh! Don't start that shit please. That was my Grubhub delivery, fool!" I spat holding up the bag of food that I had in my hands so that he could clearly see it. "You don't see this big ass brown bag in my hand?"

"Just making sure cause I know how your ass is. Did you get me something to eat too?"

"I don't know what you mean by that. How am I exactly?"

"You know how you are," Dexter taunted as we walked inside.

"Obviously, you know more than I do about myself, so please tell me how I am. What are you trying to say?" I asked as I closed then locked my front door. "I sure hope you didn't come over here to be on some bullshit. I'm really not up for all of that. I was having a pretty good day you know."

"I'm not on no bullshit. I'm just saying, you always in some other nigga's face. Don't act like that shit ain't facts."

"Kinda like how you be always in your girl's face?"

"Man whatever! What'd you get to eat?"

"I bought MYSELF some Chipotle."

"Damn it's like that? You couldn't get ya boy something to eat? You knew I was coming over."

"Well, I ordered my food before I knew you were coming, duh!"

"Yeah aight. Why you trippin' so hard?" Dexter asked as he followed me into the kitchen. I made sure to put a little extra twist in my hips knowing he was more than likely staring at my ass. "You must need some act right. Is that what it is? You missin' this big dick?"

"Nigga please!" I yawned, trying to act unfazed.

I wasn't missin' his dick, not by a longshot, but I'd be lying if I said he didn't have some good peen.

Walking up behind me, he wrapped one of his hands around my waist pulling me closer to him then slid his hand into the front of my lounging pants. I didn't have on any underwear so my shit was swangin' and hangin'.

"Put the food down," he instructed as he started stroking my shit. "Let's go in the room so I can take care of this. You can eat when we done."

"I'm starvin' let me get just one bite," I retorted, playing hard to get. I loved it when a man took control and ordered me around; in a sexual way of course.

"You picking that food over this dick?" Dexter asked, pressing his hardened monster against my ass. Fuck it, he had me. I was a sucka for a big dick.

"My food gone be cold though," I pouted, turning around then unbuckling his pants to release his beast. It was such a beautiful beast too.

"I'll buy you more once we done handling business."

"Okay bet."

Looking down at his monster as it stood at attention, I licked my lips. I dropped to my knees ready to take him into my mouth, but he stopped me.

"Hold up, let's go to the room first."

Doing as I was told, I led the way to my bedroom, preparing myself mentally for a couple more rounds of some good, hardcore fucking and sucking.

Justin

I made it home not even ten minutes before my wife did. God was on my side because I needed to jump in the shower. If she would have made it home before me I would have been fucked royally. The last thing I needed was for her to smell sex on me. I didn't know about everybody, but the smell of sex and the smell of workout sweat were two totally different smells. If I could smell myself, I knew without a doubt Ava would have smelled me. Hauling ass to our bedroom as fast as I could, I stripped out of my clothes then jumped into the shower.

As I was showering, Ava walked into the bathroom. "Hey baby, just wanted to let you know I was home."

"Hey baby girl! How was work?"

"It was fine. Today was pretty easy. Now tomorrow is going to be a different story. My schedule is booked with meetings. I texted you, how come you didn't text me back?"

"Uh... I'm sorry babe, I didn't even notice. I mean, I didn't see it. I was at the gym and didn't have my phone on me."

"Oh okay. Well, I'ma go get dinner started. I'm surprised you didn't cook."

"Yeah, I didn't get a chance to. I kinda got a late start at the gym. For it to be the middle of the day, it was packed. You know Mondays at the gym be packed from the time it opens 'til it closes."

When she didn't reply, I figured she had walked out of the bathroom. I finished washing off then stepped out of the shower. As I reached for my dry towel, I looked in the mirror and noticed a hickey on my chest. It was small but still noticeable. I wasn't sure if Ava put it there or if I had gotten it from my lover. Things got a little hot and heavy today since it had been a while since we got to spend time together.

"FUCK!" I said out loud, rushing into the bedroom so that I could get dressed. Being careless gone get my ass in some trouble, I didn't want Ava to see it just in case she wasn't the one who put it there. "Shit! Shit!"

Once I was done getting dressed, I headed to the kitchen to help Ava cook dinner. I should have gotten home earlier, so that I could have dinner done for her, especially since I was off all day and it was her first day back to work. It was the least I could do. Plus, the last thing I needed was for her to start getting suspicious and shit. To be such a beautiful woman, she had some major issues with being insecure.

She could sometimes be too observant. The shit was aggravating as hell but it kept me on my toes. I knew that cheating on my wife was fucked up on my part, but I couldn't help myself. Choosing to settle down and marry her was solely for her. I only proposed because I didn't want to lose her. I loved my wife, but she could never fully satisfy me no matter how hard she tried.

"Hey baby, give your hubby some suga," I greeted Ava as I stepped into the kitchen and walked up to her.

Wrapping my arms around her, we started kissing. I made sure to kiss her as sensual as I possibly could because I felt bad about not having dinner done for her. My nerves were getting the best of me and had me feeling bad and guilty. The least I could do was show her a little attention. Plus, it kept her from being suspicious. Ava loved attention and if I were to start slacking on giving it to her, she'd start her complaining making sure to let me know. Since things had been going so good, I wanted to keep it that way for as long as possible.

"You betta stop before you get something started," she said breaking away from my embrace then going back to gathering all of the stuff she needed to make dinner. "You smell so damn good."

"Thank you, baby. So, what you cooking? Or shall I say, what we gonna cook?"

"I was thinking grilled steaks, baked potatoes and some corn on the cob. While the food is on the grill, I'll bake the potatoes in the oven."

"That sounds good. Let me go get the grill started while you season the meat and shuck the corn."

Opening the patio door that led out to the backyard where our barbeque grills were, I went to the shed and pulled out all the stuff I needed to get the charcoal grill started. We had two grills, a propane grill and a charcoal grill. Ava usually cooked on the propane grill. She hated using the charcoal grill. The last time she tried to get it started she damn near burned all the hair off her head.

She put too much lighter fluid on the coals and when she went to put fire to them, the whole grill engulfed in flames. The shit shot so high and so quick that she didn't get a chance to back up fast enough and some of her hair caught on fire. She was pissed OFF. Once I saw that she was okay, I laughed for days behind it. So now, all the grilling was on me. We had the propane grill as option B for her for days I wasn't home and she wanted to grill.

Once I got the grill started, I cleaned it off then headed back into the house to get the meat. Ava was still seasoning the meat, so I went ahead and put the potatoes in the oven, that way they would be done by the time the steaks were ready. Baked potatoes took fucking forever to cook. Getting the grill fork and tongs, I grabbed the tray of food then headed back outside. As I was putting the food on the grill, Ava came outside and sat in one of the lawn chairs that were near the grill.

"I made you some ice water baby. It's hot as hell out here today."

"Thanks, yeah it's a scorcher."

"So how was your day? What else did you do besides go to the gym?" Ava asked.

"Shit nothing really. Like I said, I had a late start getting to the gym because I got wrapped up into this episode of the First 48."

"You actually found an episode you haven't seen already?"

"Nah," I chuckled, "it was a rerun, but a good one." I lied knowing good and well that wasn't the case.

Ava sometimes liked to ask questions like she was an interrogator. That was one of the things that I didn't particularly care for about her. I hated to be questioned, especially when I knew that I had been up to no good. Plus with her, I could never tell if she was questioning me just to be doing it or if it was because she was suspecting that I was up to no good.

"I talked to my sister and Shane today."

Thank God she brought up something else.

"Oh yeah, what's been going on with them?" I asked.

"My sister is crazy busy with work and Shane is Shane," she chuckled.

I didn't say anything as I took a long drink from the cup of water that she gave me. All of a sudden, I was thirsty as hell.

"I invited Shane over this weekend since you have to work."

"You did. What do y'all two have planned?"

"Nothing much, we're just going to catch up."

"You know how I feel about you and Shane hanging out."

"We haven't talked or seen each other since the wedding," she complained.

"Y'all are just two peas in a pod, huh? I truly don't see what y'all have in common."

"You know that's my bestie. I don't know why you don't like us hanging out."

"Probably because Shane is single and loves to mingle. You're married now. You need to start hanging with people that match your swag more. A married woman don't need to be hanging out with someone that is single and in the streets like he is."

"Oh really? What about you and Tate?" Ava countered.

"What about Tate?"

"He's single."

"He is newly single for one. And, Tate and I have been friends since the sandbox. Big difference between you and Shane," I said.

"I don't think it is."

"I guess we just gone agree to disagree on it then."

"You don't have anything to worry about. I love you and only you. Shane may like to mingle, but I don't be on that. Plus, he is coming here. It's not like we're going out to the club or something," Ava said as she came and stood next to me, looking at the meat on the grill. "Gosh that smells so good. I love me some grilled steak and you make them so perfect too!"

"Thanks baby."

"Speaking of Tate, have you talked to him since the wedding?" Ava asked.

"Actually no, I haven't. His work schedule is just as crazy as mine so you know how that goes."

"Yeah I know. I hate your work schedule, that and the fact that your job is so dangerous. It rattles my nerves when you're at work. I'm always worried hoping that nothing happens to you."

"Ain't nothing going to happen to me baby. I've been fighting fires for years and ain't nothing happened to me yet."

"I know but still. I'm not looking forward to not being with you. I've gotten used to us being together all day."

"You mean you've gotten spoiled." I laughed. "This has been my schedule since you've known me. You will be just fine. Plus your boy is coming over so you'll be A-Oh-Kay."

"I'm not talking about this weekend. I gotta get the next two days first."

"Well, it's really not that bad and it goes by fast. You gotta work so you'll only be spending the nights alone," I reasoned.

"I know but still. I hate being home alone. We need to get a dog or something-"

"Oh, hell nah! Nope," I interrupted her. "I ain't trying to be chasing after no stankin' ass dog!"

"Ahhh come on babe! I could use the companionship when you're not here."

"Then what happens on the days that I'm home. Nah man! I really ain't trying to have no dog running around here shitting all over the place and tearing shit up."

"Will you at least think about it?"

"Hmmm, let me think..." I paused for a few minutes then answered her. "There, I thought about it. Nope, the answer is still no."

"I thought firefighters liked dogs."

"You watch too much TV babe. That's a myth and very cliché."

"Just think about it. You know what they say, happy wife happy life, right?"

"Shit my life and wife gone be just fine dog or no dog. Hell, in my opinion it will be better with no dog." I laughed causing Ava to laugh too.

"You're a mess!" She giggled.

Once the steaks and corn were done, I took them off the grill and put them on the plate that Ava had brought out. She took the food into the house as I closed the top on the grill. When I got back in the kitchen, Ava was just taking the potatoes out of the oven.

"Are they done?" I asked.

"Yeah, I put the oven on broil so that it wouldn't take forever. You only had it on 350, so they would have still be cooking if I would have left them on that."

"Girl you know you smart. See, beauty and brains. That's why I love yo ass."

"You play too much." Ava chuckled as we both made our plates.

As I sat down at the kitchen table to eat, she fixed us both some sweet tea with ice, then joined me at the table.

"Thank you, baby," I said, picking up the glass of sweet tea and taking a sip. "Ouu wee that is some good ass tea."

"Gold Peak is the best. Baby this steak is so good. I swear you grill steak better than a steakhouse."

"Thanks baby."

We sat the rest of the time in silence while we ate. Occasionally, I glanced over at her and for a slight moment, I started to feel guilty for cheating on my wife. I loved her so much and honestly couldn't see my life without her in it. I just couldn't help myself. I knew that if she had any idea about what I really was up to today, she would never forgive me. And if I were her, I probably wouldn't be able to forgive myself either.

Once we were done eating, I cleaned the kitchen while Ava went to take a shower. While she was in the bedroom getting dressed, I sat in the family room and turned the TV on. *Deadliest Catch* was on, so I decided to watch it. As I sat there I figured I'd text my boy Tate to see how he was doing.

Me: What's up my boi

Tate: What up fool

Me: Shit. You free this week to meet up

Tate: I'm off Thursday

Me. Bet me too. I'll hit you up. Later

Tate: Later bro

Just as I finished texting Tate, Ava came prancing into the family room looking sexier than a motherfucker. Too bad I was worn completely out, otherwise, I would have jumped her bones on sight.

"Damn babe, you looking like a snack," I complimented, taking in the pastel pink and black lingerie she was wearing.

Ava was a very curvaceous woman. She had curves in all the right places and that lingerie she had on was hugging her body just right!

"I was thinking more like dessert," Ava responded as she straddled my lap.

Taking one of her hands, she reached under my shirt and started rubbing on my chest.

Kissing my neck, she started getting carried away and started sucking.

"Come on bae. You know I have to work tomorrow. I don't want to be walking around with a hickey on my neck."

"I'm not gonna give you a hickey silly. Hickeys are for teenagers." She giggled then continued, "I was just kissing on you. You smell like a mix of barbeque and cologne." She chuckled.

"Shit, let me go take another shower right quick then."

Fuck! That meant the hickey that was on my chest more than likely didn't come from her. Damn it!

Getting up from the couch, I headed to the bedroom to take my third shower of the day. Once I was done, I put on a pair of boxer briefs and a t-shirt then got in the bed. Looking at the clock, it was a little past nine and I needed to be up at three to get to work by four.

"I thought you were coming back to watch TV with me?" Ava asked as she joined me in our bedroom.

"Sorry babe. I didn't realize it was this late. I need to get to bed so I can get to work on time in the morning. The last thing I need is to be late on my first day back."

"Dang, I was looking forward to some cuddling."

"Come here, I'll hold you while we sleep." I yawned.

As sexy as she was looking, she was damn lucky I was sexed out for the day. My dick and balls were drier than the Sahara Desert. To say I was drained would be an understatement.

Ava climbed into bed and snuggled next to me. Laying her head on my chest, she picked up the remote for the TV and turned to one of her girly shows while I drifted off to sleep.

Chapter Three

Ava

Thursday

Hearing my alarm go off jolted me out of the deep sleep I was in. Snatching my phone off of my nightstand and hitting *Dismiss*, wanting to throw my phone across the room, I went ahead and got up. I knew that if I would have hit *Snooze*, I would have for sure overslept. It felt like I had just gone to sleep. I was beat and my body was sore from all of the lovemaking Justin and I had last night when he got home from work. We pulled a late night of Netflix and chillin'. Well, more like Netflix and sexing and right now, I was paying for it.

"Good morning babe." Justin chuckled.

Damn near jumping out of my skin then turning to face him, Justin slapped me across the ass just as I was about to walk into the bathroom that was connected to our bedroom.

"Damn it! You almost scared the life out of me J!!"

"My bad baby," he said then busted out laughing at me. "What you so jumpy for?"

"I didn't think you were in the room when I saw that you weren't in bed. I didn't even see you standing there. For Christ's sake! You could have given me a heart attack!"

"Really babe? Who else would be standing in our bedroom at five in the morning?"

"See, this is why we need a dog. A dog wouldn't have allowed for you to scare me like that." I laughed back at him.

"Oh, so you want a dog so you can train him to attack me? Ah hell nah! Now you really not about to get no dog. I almost considered that shit too." Justin continued to crack up laughing.

I'm sure I was looking a mess with my hair all over my head and sleep still in my eyes. I wasn't much of a morning person, unlike him.

"Of course, I wouldn't train our dog to attack you, silly! But I do want a dog because it will provide another layer of protection, especially on days when you're not home."

"What do you feel you need protection from?" Justin asked, stepping into the bathroom with me as I jumped into the shower.

"I have no reason in particular. I just would like the security that it would provide as well as championship."

"We haven't had a dog in all this time. Plus, we have an expensive ass security system that I pay a pretty penny for every month, babe. You straight, ain't shit about to happen to you."

"You don't know that to be factual. Because of your work hours, it's not hard for a criminal to pick up on the pattern of when your home or not. A criminal can easily figure that out and come up in here on me."

"Girl what is wrong with you this morning?!" Justin busted out laughing. "That's it! No more crime investigation shows for yo ass! You watch way too much TV babe."

"That's not funny J! Seriously though!"

"Look, if having a dog is something that you really feel you need, then I'll consider it."

"Stop playin'... for real?" I all but shouted.

I got so excited I almost slipped in the tub.

"You straight in there?"

"Yeah, I'm cool. I almost busted my ass, but I'm straight." I laughed out of embarrassment.

That was the one thing that I hated about our shower. It was so slippery! A bitch could really break something if I wasn't careful. Also, where most showers had a shower curtain hanging, that side of our shower was made of glass. So you could clearly see into the shower.

"I thought I was going to have to jump in there and catch you for a minute." Justin laughed.

"You're just full of jokes and giggles this morning."

"Consider me almost scaring the... as you say, life out of you, that's the least I can do is get you a dog. But you gon' have to take care of it and clean up after the dog. That means you're going to have it walk it so it ain't shitting all up in the house."

"I know and I will."

"That's what you say now. We'll see once we get a dog... I have a feeling I'ma be the one stuck having to walk it and clean behind it."

"I promise you won't be. Except for the days that I'm at work and you're home. I mean, that's a given though."

"I really like it just being me and you, but for you I'm trying to be understanding."

"Thanks babe. I appreciate you for understanding." I felt like part of the reason why Justin gave into us getting a dog was because I kept it real and told him that I felt unsafe being home alone. "I just know you not up in here taking a dump! JUSTIN!"

"What?! We's married nah!"

"That's so nasty! You should be shame, for real." I laughed but was serious. He could have at least waited until I got out of the shower to take a shit. "Why didn't you wait 'til

I got out to do that. I don't want to be smelling like your shit."

"I was on my way to the bathroom first. You in the shower, you not gonna smell like shit. Yo ass is crazy babe."

"So nasty!" I laughed.

Finishing up in the shower, I grabbed my dry towel off the towel heating rack. Going into our walk-in closet, I dried off then found something to wear to work. Heading back into the bedroom, I put on some baby oil then got dressed.

Just as I was almost done, Justin walked out of the bathroom into our bedroom.

"Coming out feelin' about 10 pounds lighter," he said as he rubbed his stomach.

"You have way too much energy this morning. What are you so jovial about?"

"I'm still high off the lovemaking we had last night." Walking up to me and into my space, he grabbed a chunk of my butt then kissed me on the lips. "You did yo thang last night baby."

"So did you. You better stop 'cause I can't be late to work."

"Okay, I'll stop for now."

"I promise later you can have all the kisses you want."

Kissing him one last time, I grabbed my purse, more like tote and cellphone. I knew if I stayed a minute longer another kiss would lead to other things. My husband and I were so in love we couldn't keep our hands off of one another. We had come such a long way. There for a minute we almost didn't make it. Before we got married, Justin started acting funny toward me, even the sex had changed; then things got really bad after that.

He stayed gone more than he was home on his days off, leaving me alone all the time. I had become miserable and lonely. I felt like we were ships passing in the night. We were so distant with each other that I started to suspect he was cheating with some floozy. Then when I would confront him about it, he would always say that he was with his best friend Tate.

Tate and Justin grew up together and were the best of friends. Tate was a very handsome guy that couldn't keep a girl to save his life. His mom was Egyptian and his dad was white. Tate was gorgeous! When Justin and I went to Thanksgiving dinner one year at Tate's house, I had the chance to meet Tate's parents. They were the sweetest couple... his parents definitely were couple goals. Tate was an EMT, his work schedule was similar to Justin's and often times, they would have some of the same days off.

Tate would either be over at our house or Justin would be at his. I loved Tate but it had become way too much. Some days I just wanted to chill with my man without having to share him with Tate, so them hanging out ALL of the time became a major turn off to me. When I told Justin how lonely I was feeling, he switched up and fought for our relationship. Had it not been for that, we would have never gotten married.

Heading to the kitchen, I made my daily cup of coffee thanks to Justin. It was routine for him to get up and start the coffee the mornings he would be home. I truly appreciated that. I was not a morning person in the least bit, so coffee was essential for me. Just as I finished and was heading to the garage, Justin came into the kitchen.

"See you later babe," he said, giving me a sweet kiss on the lips.

"Later J."

Heading into the garage and getting into my car, I began my trek heading to work. I called my sister for my *on the way to work morning* call.

"Good morning sissy!"

"Hey sis! How you feeling this beautiful morning?" Dawn asked, answering the phone sounding like she was out of breath.

"I feel great, but what's up with you? You straight over there?"

"What you mean?"

"Why you breathing so hard?" I chuckled. "Let me guess... you running late, ain't you?"

"Stop!" Dawn laughed. "I'm walking out the door now."

"Damn shame. Some stuff never changes."

"Period, sis," Dawn responded causing me to chuckle.

"What you got going on this weekend?"

"Nothing much. Why, what's up?"

"Justin works Friday and Saturday, so if you're free you should come by."

"I just might. I miss our sister nights."

"I do too. Shane is supposed to come over Saturday too."

"Oh okay. I just might come over. Shane is funny to hang around. It's just something about him that doesn't sit right with me. Other than that, he cool. His ass is funny as fuck I know that." Dawn giggled.

"Shane is a straight fool." I laughed along with her. "That's why I love him so much. He is a fun time for sure. I don't know why you always say it's something about him you don't like though. I swear he is super loyal and has always been a great friend to me. He's the only other person that I consider my bestie besides you. He can be a handful at times, but I love his crazy butt."

"It's just a feeling I get whenever he is around. It has nothing to do with his choice of lifestyle, to each their own, but it's just a gut feeling. Just remember, that's YOUR friend. I'm cool with him on the strength of you and that's all that it could ever be with him and I."

"Ugh, you so aggy sissy." I giggled. "Do you have a packed schedule today?"

"Yassss, Thursdays are my busiest days. Folks be wanting to get in before the weekend crowd."

"Better you than me. I don't see how you can stand on your feet all day doing people's hair."

"Shit, I don't see how you can be locked in a building with hundreds of teenagers all damn day. Better you than me!" Dawn retorted causing us both to laugh.

"Touche' sissy, touche`! Well, I do hope you can come Saturday. I need you to do a silk wrap for me."

"Oh, so that's why your butt inviting me over."

"No it's not. I miss hanging with you first, but it would be perfect and just in time for my hubby to get home too. Lord knows I done sweated my poor hair out."

"TMI sis! You know I'll hook you up. I know you hate going to the shop to get your hair done."

"I absolutely hate it. The beauty of having you for a big sis is I can get home visits."

"Girl, you a mess." Dawn laughed. "Well let me call to the shop. I need to let them know I'm almost there. And I need to tell Jackie she can start washing out my client's hair so she can be ready for me to start as soon as I get there."

"Okay sissy, love you."

"Love you too. Talk to you later."

After hanging up with Dawn, I made it to work. Parking then heading into the building, Kevin of course opened the front door and held it for me, just he did every morning.

"Good morning."

"Good morning Kevin. Have a good day," I replied as I walked into the building.

He normally would respond and make a little small talk or compliment me, but ever since I told Kevin that I had gotten married, he seemed a bit distant with me. I was used to him being more talkative and somewhat flirty. But lately, all he said was good morning. I guess that was a good thing because Kevin was a handsome man. Even though I loved my husband, I didn't want to put myself in a position that I couldn't find my way out of with Kevin. I guess Kevin was just being respectful.

When Justin and I went through our rocky patch and I was feeling lonely, I would feed into Kevin's flirting but in a discreet way. Being mindful to the fact that we were around teenagers was a must. Our flirting was innocent, platonic in a sense, but I would be lying if I didn't like the attention that he'd give me. I just never let things get to a level above playful flirting, especially working in a high school. I would never risk getting caught being inappropriate with a fellow co-worker at work. Once Justin and I got back on track, I eased up a bit from Kevin, but still entertained small talk with him. But now, he seemed to be acting a bit standoffish.

Making it to my office, I logged into the computer and settled in, ready to get my day started.

Justin

"Man I needed that." I breathed out heavily after busting a large load into my hand.

"Me too, shit. It's been a minute," Tate said as he laid back on the bed on his back stretching out. "Can you hand me a wash rag out the closet?" he asked holding his load of cum in his hand.

Going into the bathroom first to wash my hands then to the linen closet that was right outside of his bedroom, I grabbed a washrag for him as well as one for myself. Handing him one of the washrags so that he could wipe himself off, I headed into his bathroom to take a shower. Tate was not only my best friend from childhood, he was someone that I engaged in a sexual relationship with. No one knew about us having sex with one another except us. Back when we were in middle school, high school and even college, we both were athletes and hung around nothing but jocks. As masculine as we both came across to people, no one would have ever guessed that we were sleeping with each other.

Tate and I had a special connection and understanding. He dated women just as I did and we both were fine with that. Neither one of us ever got jealous with each other regarding the women we dated. Tate was the best man in my wedding, and very supportive of me and Ava's relationship and marriage. I believe that Tate was more bi-sexual than I was because he struggled more with keeping a woman than I did. It was almost like he preferred sex with me over having sex with women and to some degree, I could understand it because I felt the same way in a sense.

I loved being intimate with Ava, but sex with her was no match to having sex with a man in my opinion. Even though he never discussed it with me, I knew that he was sleeping with other men. We just never openly discussed it with one another. Just as Tate wasn't the only man I had slept with I didn't expect to be the only man in his life. The difference between he and I was that I was able to maintain a relationship with my wife, but Tate always struggled with his identity. Probably because he had more at risk than I did.

His older brother and dad were very homophobic. Tate had no choice but to hide his true identity and put on a façade by dating women to suffice them. I wouldn't even want to imagine the reaction that he would have gotten from them had they known that he was bi-sexual. Then all of our friends were manly men, I didn't think any of them would have been open to me and Tate's sexual desires and preferences, so as a result, we both vowed to never tell anyone our secret no matter who it was... including my wife.

I loved my wife more than anything in the world, but when it came to being 100% sexually satisfied with her, I wasn't. No matter how many times in a day she and I would fuck or how much foreplay we'd have, I was always left feeling completely unsatisfied with her. I knew that if I had told her that I was bi-sexual, she would not have been open to it or understanding.

The only other person that knew about me being sexual with men was my mother. Although she somewhat accepted it, it unfortunately caused a big disconnect between me and her. Back when I was in high school, Tate had spent the night at my house as he did numerous times. We'd wait 'til we thought that everyone was asleep then we'd start experimenting on each other. Well this one day, he and I were in my bedroom watching movies and once we thought everyone was asleep, we started messing around.

He started giving me oral pleasure and my mom had come to my room. Usually, she would knock before opening my bedroom door, but this day she just opened the door and caught us in the act.

To say that we were all embarrassed would be an understatement. I begged her not to tell my dad about it because he would have kicked both me and Tate's ass. Plus, my dad and Tate's dad were very good friends and shared the same opinion about gay relationships, especially when it came to two men being together. To me, whenever he would speak negatively about gay relationships, he spoke the worst about two men wanting to be together than he did about two women. My mom promised me that she wouldn't tell my dad, but it instantly changed the connection that she and I once had.

At least that was the way that it felt to me. My mom was the one that would always point out to me that I needed to experiment more with the women that I dated because she felt that I was just going through a phase. But that wasn't the case. Wanting to have sex with men was more than just a phase for me. It was more like a desire and lifestyle choice then a phase. My mom claimed she didn't judge me, but after that day she became less open for me and Tate to hang out. She stopped letting him spend the night and didn't let me stay the night at his house.

The more that Tate and I had sex together the more I grew to crave it. I was able to improvise when it came to my needs because I had more than one male lover. Whereas with Tate, I was the only man he felt comfortable with having a sexual relationship with, at first. He made it a point to portray himself as a ladies' man by dating a lot of women, but I knew he was doing it as a cover up. That was why it was always so hard for him to maintain a relationship with a woman. Just like with me, a woman didn't fully satisfy us.

Tate and I started to have sex when we were teenagers. It was something that just happened one day completely out of the blue and on mutual terms. I remember when I was younger, I would always be curious about what it would be like to have sex with a man. I just never acted on it until he and I tried it out. Considering that we both were athletes, being gay or wanting to sleep with a guy was just something that was not tolerated. The ridicule that would come with people finding out about a person's sexual desires could be frightening, especially when you come across as a strong, tough jock or family and friends that were clearly homophobic.

Clearly Tate was just as curious about sleeping with a man as I was because like I said, from day one our hook-ups we had been on mutual terms. I remember the first day we slept together. It was a Friday evening and I was spending the night at his house. We had football practice after school that day then we both walked to his house afterward. On the way there, we were sharing stories about the girls we both were talking to with another guy,

Jason that was also on the football team with us.

He was walking with us because he lived next door to Tate. Sharing stories about the different chicks that we'd hooked up with was very common amongst our group of friends. In our group, the one with the most hook-ups or prettiest girls checking for them were always looked upon as THE MAN and because of it, they would get major props. And who wouldn't want to be the man.

Tate and I were always two of the guys in our group of friends that all the popular girls would flock to. We were hardcore jocks that could basically have any chick that we wanted. Well, that particular day, I was telling Tate and Jason about a girl named Jenny, who just so happened to be the captain of the varsity cheerleading team. We were juniors in high school and Jenny was a senior, who was in love with me. Long story short, she and I exchanged numbers and had hooked up one day after school and she gave me oral. I was telling Tate and Jason about Jenny and I, bragging of course, as they gave me my props for hooking up with one of the most popular girls in the school and who was a year older than us.

Once we got to Tate's, Jason went his way and Tate and I went inside his house. We both were starving, so we popped some pizza rolls in the oven. As I waited for them to cook, Tate went to take a shower and change. We both were very sweaty and funky from practice. By the time he was finished taking a shower, the pizza rolls were ready, so I took them out of the oven then went to Tate's room to let them know that they were done.

"Hey, I took the pizza rolls out of the oven. Can I get a dry towel and washrag? I'm not feeling the B.O. my body is giving off right now." I laughed, roasting on myself because I knew I had to be funky by the way that I had just been sweating.

"Thanks bro. The towels are in the hall closet," Tate responded as he stood in his bedroom with his bath towel wrapped around his waist. Seeing him standing there wet, caused a weird feeling to wash over me. It made me check myself because that was the point when I realized I was attracted to Tate, physically.

We were home alone, his older brother was away at college and both of his parents were at work. His parents didn't care about me being at their house without them there because like I said, we grew up together and had been friends for years. If you saw me you saw Tate and vice versa. It was very common for us to spend the night to each other's house often.

Heading to the hallway, I grabbed the towels that I needed then walked back into his room to take my clothes off so that I could take a shower. As I was getting undressed I kept catching Tate looking at me weird. At the same time, I couldn't help but to steal a few glances of him as he stood in his room naked as the day he was born drying himself off. It wasn't uncommon for us to be naked around each other.

The whole football team showered and dressed in front of one another in the locker room and all we did was walk around naked in the locker room. With that being said, it was another reason why it would have been looked down upon us had our friends known about Tate and I sleeping together. I was sure it would have caused for them to feel a type of way about us.

There was this one kid that wrestled on our high school wrestling team that was gay and all of the jocks at the school would talk about him and poke fun at him. I remembered on more than one occasion during football season, wrestling practice would start up because wrestling season started right after football season was over. So, there were times when the wrestling team would be in the locker room at the same time as the football team and the majority of the guys on the football team felt a type of way about being naked in front of the dude that was gay.

I used to feel so bad for him, so I just never made fun of him and I didn't encourage it when people would pick on him in front of me. It was vital for both me and Tate's popularity status that no one knew about what we had going on.

Getting weird feelings and sensations running through my body and mind as I watched Tate, I left out of his room and headed to take a shower. Stepping into the shower, I couldn't hide the fact that I had a hard-on. That had never happened before, but today for some reason, seeing him naked had me really feeling some type of way. Instantly, I had become horny but knew I had to control my desires. So, taking my hard dick in my hands, I jagged my shit off in the shower as I fantasized about having sex with Tate. I couldn't believe how hard I had cum from doing that.

When I was done showering, I headed back into Tate's room and thankfully, he wasn't in there. I assumed he was in the kitchen eating. After changing into a pair of clean basketball shorts and a t-shirt that I had in my gym bag, I headed to the kitchen. By this time, I felt like my stomach was touching my back. I was so hungry.

Tate was sitting in the family room on the sofa watching *13 Reasons Why* on Netflix while eating. So, I grabbed a plate out of one of the cabinets in the kitchen, fixed my plate and joined him on the sofa. As we were sitting there watching TV, he asked me a question that changed the direction of our relationship forever.

"Can I ask you a question and you not think or look at me crazy?"

"What's up?"

"Have you ever thought about having sex with a dude?"

"Come again?" I asked, almost choking on a pizza roll.

"Never mind, it was a stupid question."

"No question is stupid. Have you thought about it before?" I asked, answering his question with a question.

"Sleeping with a dude?" he asked as if he needed to make sure I was asking him that when he was the one that initiated the conversation.

"Yeah," I responded.

There were a few moments of silence before he answered me.

"I would be lying if I said I didn't. I ain't gone lie, sometimes when I watch porn, I check out a few dude on dude action." I was speechless because I had done the same thing. I just never told anyone. I didn't know how to respond because the air and tension in the room had shifted. "It's no biggie, I was just curious about it is all."

"You don't have to feel embarrassed because I have been curious as well," I responded, I could tell that Tate was feeling embarrassed by my reaction to his question just from the look on his face. "I have checked out a few dude on dude porn videos also. I would be lying if I said I never thought about it."

"Do you think you could ever fuck a dude?"

"I mean, I don't know." I had just fantasized about him and I fucking in his shower, but I wasn't about to tell him that. "How about you?"

"I don't know. You know how my brother and dad are. They're really not open to dudes with dudes. You know my Uncle Jim is gay and he and my dad don't get along at all."

"So are you saying you think you might be gay?"

"Nah, I'm not saying that. I'm just saying that I have been curious about what it would be like to be with a dude. I'm not saying I want to be in a full fledge relationship with a dude."

"Oh, but you would be open to experimenting with one?"

"That's the thing, I don't know. Like, I don't feel that way when we're around our boys, but I'd be lying if I said I haven't felt that way around you."

Almost choking on the pizza roll I had just popped in my mouth, I was speechless. Tate admitting that he had thought about him and I having sex before was news to me. The fact that I too had thought about fucking him instantly made me feel some type of way. All I knew was that one thing led to another and Tate and I ended up in his bedroom experimenting with each other's body and the satisfaction that I got from it was no comparison to how I would feel being with a girl.

We both ended up enjoying fucking one another more than we ever imagined we would and from that day forward, he and I maintained a secret sexual relationship.

Yesterday, Tate ended up being off from work, so we spent all day together, and here I was again at his house today. It was almost like Tate and I were addicted to one another. Since we knew each other's bodies like the back of our own hands, we both knew what each other needed to satisfy one another. He and I never kissed, but we did perform oral sex on one another and we both gave and received when it came to fucking on one another.

A normal sex session between us would be us doing oral on each other in the 69 position then we'd take turns having intercourse. We always pulled out, never cumming in each other's mouth or ass. That was something that we both agreed to being off limits from the very start.

I was cool with it because I was able to fulfill that desire with my other male lover. Tate didn't know that I was seeing another man, and I never thought to tell him. As far as I knew, I was the only man he was sleeping with so it was like an understanding that the two of us had that we'd be each other's only male sex partner. Since I had broken that pact, I didn't want to say anything to him because I didn't want it to affect what we had going on or our friendship.

Tate and I hadn't seen each other since my wedding day, so we definitely were enjoying each other's company for the last two days. It was like we couldn't get enough of each other. He liked for me to tell him about the sex I'd have with Ava, it was a turn on for him. Then from there we'd fuck on each other all day long. I was scheduled to work the next two days and I was going to go in for a half day Sunday for one of my co-workers that had a death in his family. My typical work schedule was two days on and one day off, but this coming week was going to be kind of hectic... not just for me, but for Tate as well, so we had to get as much as we could out of each other today.

Noticing that it was almost 11pm, I had to head home. I knew that Ava would be in her feelings because I had stayed out late for the last two nights. I had fallen back into my old routine of hooking up with my lovers and spending the majority of my time off with them this week. I didn't think it was that big of a deal since Ava had started back to work this week and her days had been pretty busy. Plus, I felt like the little break from her was needed because we had been glued to each other since the wedding. She may not have felt that we needed space, but I surely did.

Making promises to meet up on our next day off together, I headed to my car so that I could make my way home. I felt like I was floating on cloud nine. The sex from these last two days had me on such a high. I noticed that I had a few missing calls from my other lover. I knew he was probably feeling some type of way since he hadn't heard from me or seen me since Monday. I was supposed to hang out with him yesterday, but since Tate was available to hook up, I chose to spend my days off with him instead.

Not wanting to get into it with him over not coming over, I figured I'd wait to call him back tomorrow if I had the time. He sometimes tended to act out when he and I didn't hook up as often as he would have liked. For now, I was going to relish in the glorious mood that Tate had me in.

Making it home at a little past 11:30pm, I saw that Ava had cooked dinner and left me a plate on the stove. Heading into our bedroom, I saw that she was sound asleep. Thank God because she and I were supposed to be chilling together tonight and I had ghosted her. I felt bad for doing her like that, but she was my wife, so she wasn't going anywhere. I knew that whenever I wanted time with her, all I had to do was initiate it and she'd comply.

Heading back into the kitchen, I heated up the plate of food she let for me in the microwave, ate, showered then got in bed with my wife so that I could go to sleep to be up on time for work in the morning.

Chapter Four

Ava

Sunday morning

The last couple of days, I had been in a funk. Justin had me feeling some type of way. This past week, he spent more time at Tate's house than he did at home with me. I was trying to be understanding because I knew they were close and liked to play the PlayStation and watch sports on TV together. They hadn't gotten to see each other after the wedding because Justin and I were honeymooning and spending as much time together as possible. Now that we were married, I thought that he was going to chill on hanging out with Tate so much.

He promised me before we got engaged that he would do better with that, but now he was starting to fall back into the old patterns that he used to have. Wednesday, I didn't feel a way about him coming home late because I kind of expected that being that he and Tate hadn't hung out for a lil minute, but when

Justin didn't get home 'til late Thursday night too, I was pissed off.

He and I were supposed to Netflix and chill, especially since we weren't going to see each other until today. Thankfully, Shane and my sister came over last night and I got the chance to get my mind off of Justin. I told them about the honeymoon and painted this picture to them both that things were never better between me and Justin because I didn't want to come off as selfish. The same way I made it a point to take the time to hang with Shane and Dawn, I knew I had to give Justin his time with his friends as well.

"Well boo, I'ma head out before the man of the house gets home. Shouldn't he be here soon?" Shane asked as he finished helping me clean the kitchen.

I had just cooked up some breakfast for the three of us. We all got stupid drunk off of the Sangria that I had made.

"Yeah, I probably should be heading out too. I have a date tonight," Dawn said grinning from ear to ear.

"Y'all don't have to rush to leave. You know Justin doesn't care about you guys being over here."

"I know, but you know how long it takes for me to get ready and I don't want to be late."

"Yeah, your ass is notoriously always running late." I chuckled. "I can't believe you're going out on a date with Tate. He is a cutie and all. I just didn't think he was your type."

"You know I love me some dark chocolate men, but Tate is a sweetheart. Well, from what I can see and from what you told me. Plus, he is a sexy ass tall glass of milk."

"He is very sexy," I agreed.

"He's aight," Shane interrupted. "He's not all that. I have seen much sexier white boys than him."

"I bet you have." Dawn laughed. "I'm excited to see where things go with me and Tate. I know that he is crazy busy like Justin with his work schedule. So far, all we have done is talk on the phone because he is always working. But I'm cool with it. I don't like guys that are clingy anyway."

"How long have y'all been talking again?" Shane asked with a disgusted look on his face. For some reason, Shane never really cared for Tate. "How did y'all even start talking in the first place?"

"Ever since the wedding actually. As much as I have seen him over here, we never really hung out before like we did the night you and Justin got married. Usually, he and Justin would be in the basement playing the game and me and you," Dawn said referring to me. "Would always be doing our own thing upstairs. But the night of the wedding, we exchanged numbers and have been talking ever since."

"Well, for what it's worth, I think y'all make a cute couple. The only thing that concerns me is that for as long as I have known him, he has never been able to keep a girlfriend."

"Mmmmm hmmmm," Shane snickered, causing me to giggle as Dawn looked at him.

"What was that for? Why don't you like Tate?" Dawn asked, taking the words I wanted to say right out of my mouth.

"It's just something about him I don't vibe with. He probably can't keep a relationship with a woman going because he's on the DL," Shane snickered.

"Why would you say that?! Maybe it's because he is a manly man and he makes you feel uncomfortable. Tate being on the DL is highly unlikely. You know his brother is anti-gay and so is his dad. I kinda think he is anti-gay too because I have heard him make a comment once or twice, but I never saw him say or do anything to you to make you feel like you do," I said trying to defend Tate.

It was no secret that Tate was a true jock and loved him some women.

"I don't know what it is. Just ignore me chile, you know how I am." Shane chuckled trying to make light of the conversation.

"Let you tell it, all men are on the DL," Dawn retorted coming for Shane.

"That's not true, for the most part. Y'all both would be surprised by how many men are on the DL. I'm saying, if anyone knows I know."

"I bet you do," Dawn remarked giving Shane a dirty look.

Things were starting to get a little heated between Dawn and Shane, so I interjected. The last thing I wanted was for my sister and bestie to be beefing when I knew that my sister didn't really care for Shane in the first place.

"If anything, I would be more concerned with why he can't keep a girl, especially now that you and him are talking. I have always considered Tate to be a player, so I would feel some type of way if he wound up doing you wrong," I said to Dawn, letting her know what she was up against.

"I hear you, but we not talking about getting married sissy. We've just been having good conversations and tonight, we're having dinner together. Like I said, we enjoyed each other's company the night of the wedding, so I guess we're just seeing where things could go. It's nothing serious."

"Well, just be careful cause I would hate to have to hurt my husband's bestie for hurting my sister."

"Why would you have to hurt my bestie for your sister?" Justin asked walking into the kitchen startling the three of us.

Looking over to Dawn, I didn't know how she felt about me sharing the news of her and Tate talking.

"Hey babe, I didn't hear you come in," I said walking up to Justin and giving him a hug and kiss.

"Hey J," Dawn said giving Justin a hug.

"How you doing, Justin?" Shane asked giving him dap.

There was a weird vibe in the room as we all just stood there.

"Welp, let me get my things so I can get home. Lord knows I have a ton to do," Dawn said.

"I'm right behind you D," Shane said as he and Dawn went into the living room to get their bags. I walked them both out as Justin left the kitchen, headed to our bedroom.

After saying goodbye to Shane and Dawn, I joined Justin in the bedroom. He was taking a shower in the master bathroom. Figuring I'd surprise him, I stripped out of my clothes and joined him in the shower.

"Hey baby, I missed you so much," I said as I started to rub his back.

He didn't turn around like he normally would, shocking me.

"I missed you too, babe. Let's switch places cause I'm all done," he responded as he stepped to the side, so that I could get in front of him.

When he stepped out of the shower, I continued to wash off as I heard him leave out of the bathroom and go into the bedroom. I just knew he was going to be all over me being that it had been some days since we last had sex. We had gone from fucking literally every day, sometimes more than once in a day, to no sex at all this week.

Once I was done in the shower, I headed back into the bedroom to get dressed. To my surprise, Justin wasn't in the room. I just knew he would be lying in bed or at least waiting for me. Deciding to wear a cute pair of black boy shorts with a crop top... my plan was to try to get my husband's attention. I heard him stirring around in the kitchen, standing there trying to decide if I should go in there with him or if I should get in the bed and watch TV until he came back into the bedroom.

I decided to wait for him in the room.

Getting in bed, I flipped through the channels while I waited for him to get done. Forty-five minutes later, he hadn't returned to the bedroom, so I got out of bed and went to see what he was up to. I found him sitting in the family room with the TV on scrolling on his phone.

"Hey babe, I thought you were coming back to the bedroom?"

"Hey bae, I'm not tired. Those pancakes that you made were bomb. Thanks for saving me a plate."

"Always babe," I replied taking a seat next to him. Out the corner of my eye, I saw that he turned slightly so that I couldn't see what he was looking at on his phone. "Is everything okay?"

"Yeah, why wouldn't it be?"

"Things just feel a little off between me and you."

"Things are fine babe. Do you have something on your mind you feel you need to get off your chest or something?"

"Do you?" I asked, finding the question a little weird.

Putting his phone down then turning to face me, he replied, "No, why are you asking me that?"

"It just seems like things are off."

"Things are all good babe. I know we haven't been spending a lot of time together, but I didn't want to wear my welcome out with you. We have been stuck to each other like Velcro so I was just giving you a little space is all."

"What do you mean by that?" I asked, feeling confused because we were married. I didn't understand what he was talking about.

"We've been spending a lot of time together since the engagement and stuff. A little time apart and a little space is not a bad thing. Everyone needs a little me time don't you think?"

"We're married J. My me time is when I'm at work and you're away at work. That's all the time I need apart from you. Lately, I'm not gone lie, I've been feeling a little neglected."

"Neglected!? Really Ava? Now you know I haven't been neglecting you. Maybe I shouldn't have spent so much time kicking it with Tate this past week, but I hadn't seen my boy in a minute because I was making you a priority," he said.

I was his wife, so he should be making me a priority all the time. If he was looking for me to feel guilty about that, he had better look for that shit somewhere else.

"I get that. I just don't want things to get like they were before. It's like you prefer to hang out with Tate than to be with me. Then when y'all hang out, it's always a late night for you and we don't get to spend any one on one time together."

"Well, I figured I'd give you a break on the dick. I had been dicking you down so much, I don't want you to get sick of me."

"Baby, I could never get sick of you. If things were to go my way, I'd have sex with you every day just like before," I admitted, and it was true. "The only days off would be when my aunt Flo comes. Other than that, I can't get enough of you," I continued as I straddled his lap. "I miss you."

"I miss you too baby."

We started kissing and one thing led to another. Before I knew it, Justin was hitting my kitty from the back on the sofa in the family room.

Justin

Hearing my wife complain about us not spending as much time together as she would have wanted over the past week was starting to aggravate the hell out of me, but the last thing that I wanted was to get into an argument with her. When she got into the shower with me, I knew what she was on, but I wasn't in the mood for all of that. I had been working for the last two days and just wanted to relax. But then she came into the family room while I was trying to chill, yapping about not wanting things to go back to how they were before I proposed to her. So, being the good husband that I was, I ended up giving in and taping her ass from the back right there in the family room on the couch.

"Whew babe, that was so good. I needed that."

"Thanks babe," I replied as I backed up off of Ava then headed for the bathroom so that I could wash myself off.

As soon as I stepped into the bathroom, Ava was on my heels.

"I gotta take a shower. I feel sticky. Care to join me?"

"Nah baby, not this time. Do you though," I said as I grabbed my washrag and started cleaning myself off at the bathroom sink. "I'm about to relax. I have to be to work early in the morning. All I'm really trying to do for the rest of the evening is chill."

"What do you mean you have to work in the morning? I thought you were off tomorrow?"

"I'm supposed to be off, but Derek and I are splitting Rob's shift tomorrow. Rob had a death in his family and needs the day off."

"Hmph, okay I guess. I'm sorry to hear that Rob had a death in his family. That was nice of you to work part of his shift for him."

"Yeah, plus I could use the overtime. My savings took a hard hit over the last few months, so I need to recoup and make as much money as I can."

"You act like we're hurting for money."

"I didn't say that. I just said I could use the overtime to build my savings account back up is all. Why are you so on edge?"

"I'm not on edge. I just don't want you to get wrapped up in all things Justin and forget that you now have a wife that enjoys and needs your attention also."

"Babe, you make it pretty hard to forget I have a wife," I rebutted then headed out of the bathroom.

This was the shit that I was talking about. Don't get me wrong, I loved my wife more than anything, I just needed my space and for some reason she couldn't understand that. I could only imagine how she would feel if she knew about the secret lifestyle I had, which was why I never intended on her ever finding out about it.

It was a little after one in the afternoon, but I was feeling beat, so I decided to lay in bed in hopes of being able to take a nap. Just as I was getting comfortable, here comes Ava, hopping in bed next to me. Grabbing the remote for the TV, she turned it on.

"Wanna watch some Netflix with me?"

"To be honest, I was hoping to take a nap." I sighed as I watched her browse through the new releases on Netflix.

"Suit yourself then. Since you don't want to watch anything, I'ma check out Good Girls to see what all the hype is about."

"Ava, sweetie pie, would it be asking too much for you to watch TV in the family room? I'm tired as hell and all I want is to be able to get some rest," I huffed as nicely as possible.

"I swear you been acting real distant lately, but it's whatever J!" Ava spat, turning the TV off then throwing the remote down hitting me on my arm with it.

I wanted to say something because I honestly didn't have a clue what she was bitching about but decided to just keep quiet instead. She was huffin' and puffin' looking silly as hell as she snatched up her cellphone then headed out of our bedroom. On her way out, she made sure to slam our bedroom door extra hard and that was when she had me about to snap out on her ass.

Snatching my cellphone off of the bedside table next to me, I decided to text Tate to see if he was home. I needed to get out of the house and away from Ava before I wound up saying or doing something that I would regret later.

Me: wyd

Tate: getting ready for a date

When Tate replied back that was when I remembered walking in on Ava talking about Tate to Shane and Dawn.

Me: with Ava's sister?

Tate: Yeah man

Me: You playing with fire man. When did y'all start kicking it?

Tate: at your wedding bro. Playing with fire how?

Me: she's my wife's sister bro. That's weird as fuck. You know how you are when it comes to women. Are you sure that you should go there with her? The last thing I need is to have any static from my wife about you and her sister

Tate: Man it's not even that serious. We're just hanging out and having fun. I don't see how it can cause any static with you and Ava. Truthfully, it has nothing to do with you or Ava

Me: Alright then bro. You know I could care less about who you kick it with, but that's my wife's sister... just do right by

her please cause you know how Ava can get

Tate: Got it... no worries

I really didn't care if Tate and Dawn kicked it. I just didn't want things to go left with them and Dawn to bring the shit to Ava. Then Ava would come to me with it. Tate was a cool dude and all but he couldn't maintain a relationship with a woman to save his soul. I knew the real reason behind why which made it even more unsettling for me that he chose Dawn of all people to kick it with. Seeing that Tate was not available, I decided to hit up my option B.

Me: Hey, you busy

S.B: How did I know that I would be hearing from you today

Me: How so

S.B: The look and the vibe you gave off this morning to start

Me: Are you home? I need to get out of the house

S.B: Yeah I'm home.

Me: Bet. I'm on my way

Getting out of bed and throwing on a Nike jogging suit with a pair of Air Force Ones, I grabbed my cellphone, wallet and keys then headed to the garage.

"Where you going, J?"

"Out!" I grunted as I walked through the kitchen heading to the garage door.

I noticed that Ava had got up from the couch and was heading toward me.

"Out where? And don't say Tate's house because he and Dawn are about to go out."

"Oh my God Ava! You doing too much babe. I swear I don't know why you enjoy nagging me like you do."

"Nagging you?! You just sent me out of our bedroom so that you could rest and not even ten minutes later, you talking about you going out. What's going on with you?"

"I just need some air."

"Why, what's wrong? Why do you feel you need to leave to get air?"

"Just leave it be Ava seriously. I can't with all of this nagging."

I was really trying hard not to gap out on her ass and hurt her feelings, but she just wouldn't let up.

"Really J! I don't want to leave it be! What is going on with you?"

"YOU!" I bellowed as loud as I could. "You're the problem!!! You're crowding and smothering the hell out of me Ava. All I want to do is chill and be left alone and you just don't get it, man!"

"It's not my intention to make you feel crowded or smothered Justin. I just enjoy being with you is all. You making me feel like you don't like being around me."

"Are you serious right now? If I didn't like being around you, I wouldn't have married your ass. I didn't realize that once we got married, if I'm not working you'd expect me to be up under you all the damn time. Distance makes the heart grow fonder. Hell you don't give me enough space to miss ya ass. I'll be back!" I spat shaking my head then went into the garage slamming the door behind me.

I hated that I had to get into it with Ava but damn! You would think that she would be just as tired of being up under me as I was of being up under her. I could tell from the look in her eyes that I had hurt her feelings, which was something that I was definitely not trying to do, but she pushed me over the cliff that time.

Hopping in my truck, I backed out of the garage then headed to get a little peace of mind.

Chapter Five

Ava

Standing there looking at the garage door after Justin walked out, making sure to slam it on his way, had me really feeling some type of way. All I wanted to do was spend a little time with my husband and he was making me feel like I was asking him to go mountain climbing in a winter snowstorm. Then for him to tell me that he was feeling smothered and I was crowding his space really struck a nerve with me. Like what did he even mean by that?! For the past week, if he wasn't at work he was hanging out at Tate's house.

Was it really too much to ask him to chill with me today? And this time, he couldn't say he was going to hang with Tate because Tate was about to go out with my sister. So now, I was really feeling concerned wondering where and who he was going to be with that was more important than I was.

I needed to vent so I decided to call Shane. I knew that my sister was more than likely busy getting ready for her date, so I didn't want to bother her. Going back into the family room, I grabbed my cellphone and called Shane up.

"Hey bestie, you missing me already?" Shane's crazy ass asked when he answered my call.

Breathing in heavily then sighing loudly, I couldn't even laugh at Shane's humor because I was feeling some type of way. "I just need someone to talk to."

"Oh my God! What's wrong bestie?"

"Justin is what's wrong. For the past week, he has been acting real distant towards me."

"How so boo?"

"If he isn't at work then he is hanging out with Tate. Then his ass gone tell me that I was making him feel smothered... what kind of shit is that though!?" I cried.

"Awww boo don't cry. Y'all just got married and now that both of y'all are back to work, you just missing him being with you all day every day is all. I get it, but you know how men can be, especially *your* man. He loves his space boo, so try not to take that personal. You knew what you were getting into when y'all got married, hunny."

"Yeah, I know and I get that, but he promised me that he was going to make us a priority. Now that we are married, he acts like he doesn't want to be bothered with me."

"Girl, you might need to take a pregnancy test cause your ass is being super emotional over nothing in my opinion. It's only been a week friend and y'all were attached to each other so tight I can see him wanting just a lil bit of space, at least enough to miss you. Y'all need to get back to y'all's normal activities, or routine I should say for a lack of better word. You still stuck in the honeymoon phase chile."

"Why are you picking his side? It must be a man thing cause you not getting how I'm feeling."

"Aht not true. I'm not picking a side boo."

"It sure sounds like you are to me cause I honestly don't think I'm being emotional. I mean, I'm emotional because I want to hang out with my husband? That's just crazy."

"Oh, trust and believe, I get where you coming from. I just think you expected things to change with you and Justin once y'all got married, but he is who he is. Some people just need their space and there is nothing wrong with that."

"True, but he said I was crowding and smothering him Shane, like really though!"

"Girl, that's just code that he needs his space is all. He probably shouldn't have put it like that, but knowing you, you probably been on his so…"

"What's that supposed to mean?"

"Just what I said boo. You know how you both can be."

"And how is that Shane? Enlighten me please."

"I just feel like you're just not over him not showing you the time and affection that he lacked before y'all decided to run off and get married. My thing is, you knew Justin liked to kick it when y'all was just dating and you didn't particularly care for it then. How did you think you would feel about it now? And please don't give me no shit about you thought he had changed cause that's just who he is."

"So him needing his space is hanging out with Tate on his off days?"

"Well not exactly, but I kinda get how he feels booski. Look, I'm not trying to pick his side but in a way I get it. I'm the same way, I hate to date men that are clingy as fuck. I don't like it. I don't like it. I don't like it. It's a major turn off to me honestly honey and Justin strikes me as the same way."

"So you're saying I'm too clingy?"

"Yai, yai, yai mamacita you not getting it. Look at it this way. You're the leading lady in his life. He goes to bed next to you every night and wakes up to you every morning. Every single thing that he does is centered around you. Is he wrong for wanting to hang with his friends for a little bit? Like, women are so much more emotional than men are. I'm sure you would be a-oh-kay with being with Justin every waking minute of the day, no breaks just Justin, Justin, Justin. But men aren't like that sweetie and right now you're taking it personal as hell. When I say that you knew what you were getting yourself into, I mean just that. If you knew he was like that why move forward and marry him? Why not find a man that wants to be around you and only you is all I'm saying?"

"I personally feel like you're putting a ten on a two with it Shane. I don't feel like I'm asking for too much. I don't expect him to be with me every waking minute of the day, but I do expect for him to put me before his friends is all I'm saying. Especially with us being married."

"Well, I'm just saying you might want to loosen the tight grip you have on him before you turn him off completely then you'll really have major problems. I don't think he meant it how you're taking it to be honest."

"I'm just not trying to be made the fool off. I just have this gut feeling that he is up to no good when he is gone all of the time."

"You gotta stop thinking like that. I highly doubt another woman is something you need to concern yourself with. You are the only woman for Justin, that is something I wholeheartedly believe sweetie."

"Thanks Shane, I appreciate that."

"No thanks needed booski. But, I hate to cut this convo short chile, but I gotta call you back a lil later. I have a little friend stopping by and I need to get myself together honey. My hair is all over my head and that ain't cute at all." Shane chuckled causing us both to laugh.

"You and your friends, I swear you always hooking up with someone, but I get it. I wish I could be coupled up right now but it's cool."

"Awww bestie, don't feel like that. You's married now and married life ain't easy chile. Just give Justin some time. Y'all gone be straight and everything will work out."

"I sure hope so friend cause I don't want things to go back to me feeling alone in a relationship again. That's definitely not what I signed up for and this time I won't tolerate it. I can be unhappy and lonely by my damn self. I shouldn't have to feel this way with a whole husband."

"I get it boo. Well, I'ma call you back later if that's cool. Ciao!"

"Yeah, that's cool. Have enough fun for both of us. I'll chat with you later. Ciao bestie."

Hanging up with Shane, I kinda felt worst than I was feeling before I called him. For him to say that I need to loosen the grip and insinuate that I was being clingy was not cool. I knew he didn't mean any harm by what he said, but he was basically siding with Justin in my opinion. It had to be a guy thing because even though I understood where he was coming from, I didn't think he was hearing me completely. I really didn't want to bother my sister, but I needed some kind of reassurance that I wasn't tripping, so I called Dawn in hopes that I would catch her before she left for her date.

"Hey sissy, I didn't expect to be hearing from you. Is everything okay?"

"Hey sis," I sighed then continued. "No, everything isn't okay. I wasn't going to call you but I need to talk."

"What's wrong? You sound like you've been crying. What happened? You were fine earlier. Who ass I gotta kick?"

"Gurl," I chuckled cause my sister stayed ready to go, especially when it came to me. "Me and Justin just had it out. He said some things that really hurt my feelings sis."

"About what and what did he say?! Was he upset about you having company when he got home?"

"No... why you asked that?"

"Cause when he walked in, he looked like he really didn't feel like being bothered. The look he gave Shane girl... why you think I hauled ass up out of there like I did."

"How did he look at him? I didn't notice it."

"Chile..." Dawn sang into the phone and I couldn't help but to giggle.

"He could care less about me having company. Hell if anything he probably wishes that y'all would have stayed being that he wasn't trying to be bothered with me."

"Why you say that? Girl what happened?"

"Long story short he basically said that I have been smothering him."

"Smothering him? How so?"

"Because I wanted us to chill together and he didn't feel like being bothered with me. Then I called Shane and told him what happened and his ass gone say I should loosen my grip and alluded to me being too clingy with Justin. He basically said I was at risk for turning J off from me and that I was being too emotional. Do you think that I'm being too emotional?"

"I'm just confused. I'm still stuck on the whole smothering thing. Why does Justin feel smothered? And PLEASE don't get me started on Shane's dramatic ass. He has a lot of nerve calling someone emotional with his over-the-top emotional ass! I'm just saying."

"Don't start. I didn't call for this to turn into a Shane bashing convo."

"That's why I say, that's your friend cause whew chile!"

"Anyway sissy, I don't even know why Justin would say that to me cause we barely been hanging out with each other since I've been back to work. I guess I just expected that on his off days he would want to spend time with me, but that hasn't been the case. Shane is saying that it's just been a week and I'm being all emotional, but I don't think that I am."

"Can I be honest with you sissy and you not get offended?"

"Of course, you can."

"It has only been a week and y'all have been with each other day in and day out and every day before that, so just give it some time. You know how men can be, especially Justin who likes to hang, kick it and play the game with his friends. I get how you're feeling. I wouldn't go so far as to say you're being emotional, clingy, smothering and whatever else was said, but there is nothing wrong with giving him a little space. If he talking about you crowding him and smothering him, I think that's just his way of saying he needs a little personal time is all. Honestly, there is nothing wrong with that. Now if he comes to you saying he needs days, weeks or months to himself, that's a different story. But a few hours or so here and there is nothing wrong with that."

"I hear you sis. So, you don't think I have anything to be worried about then?"

"Anything to worry about like what?"

"Like him cheating or wanting to spend time with another female other than me."

"Sissy are you serious?! Nah, that man ain't messing around on you. He's just being a man. The thing is it's only been a week. Now, if he continues to act distant as you say, then I'd say it's time to start panicking."

"That's true. I see your point."

"So where is Mr. Lover Man at now?"

"He left and that's another thing. When I asked him where he was going he just said 'out'. I know he ain't going to Tate's because you and Tate about to go out, so where else could he have gone?"

"Ain't no tellin'. I don't know sissy, but Tate's not his only friend so don't put too much on that. I say, fix yourself some more of that good ass sangria you made for me and your boy, have a glass or two, or three and just chill and try to relax. Enjoy the time you have to yourself."

"You're right sis. Thanks so much for calming me down. Well, I won't hold up much more of your time. I would hate to be the reason you're not ready for your date. You know how time is your worst enemy and all." I laughed feeling much better than I did when I was talking to Shane.

"Oh girl, you not holding me up at all. Any time you need to talk, you know I'm here for you. I think most times you'd rather talk to Shane instead of me cause I keep it a little too real."

"You're right about that, but today Shane kinda had me feeling some type of way."

"I have to side with him this time to a certain extent though. His delivery was off, but I wouldn't expect anything different from Shane's ass. But, the jist of what he was saying I could totally understand. I do think you need to give Justin just a little space because men can be funny acting with stuff like that. Other than that, I understand why you're nervous, but you knew how he was before y'all got married and marrying a man doesn't change their ways. If anything, they become way more comfortable than they were before, but I don't think that's the case with Justin. Don't worry yourself sissy, y'all straight."

"Okay, I won't. I guess you saying that I should ease up is conformation since you, Justin and Shane are all basically saying the same thing."

"Welp then it's conformation then."

"Enjoy your date sis. I can't wait to hear all about it in the morning."

"You know I'll let you know all about it. Talk to you in the morning. Love you."

Hanging up with Dawn, I couldn't help but to now feel bad because maybe they were right. Maybe I was being a bit extra with Justin. No wonder he snapped and left out to get some air. I just didn't know why I continued to have a feeling in the pit of my stomach that Justin's being distant was something that I should have been concerned about. Now that I thought more about it, I was probably just having flashbacks from when things were really bad between us.

Even then, I had suspected that he was cheating only to find out that whenever he said he was with Tate that was exactly where he was. Shane and Dawn were right. I knew before I married Justin that he liked to hang out, but I married him anyway. So, I was going to have to do my best to ease up off of him a little and hopefully, the uncomfortable feeling in the pit of my stomach would eventually go away.

I figured that I would take my sister's advice and pour myself a tall glass of wine and relax while I waited for Justin to get home, so I could apologize for doing the most and freaking out on him.

The Next Morning

I wished I could call into work this morning because I was exhausted as hell, but I couldn't do that to my students. I had a full schedule and tons of work to do. The kids that I was scheduled to meet with today depended on me, so I couldn't leave them hanging by not going in. The reason I was so restless was my own fault anyway. When I hung up with Dawn last night, I took her advice and fixed myself a drink and binge watched *Little Fires Everywhere* on Hulu while I waited on Justin to get back home.

Since Tate was with Dawn, I didn't expect for Justin to be gone long, but to my surprise he got in at almost three this morning. I pretended to be asleep, but I wasn't. I tried to pretend like I was asleep and not say anything because I didn't want to get into it with him, especially on a day when he had to go into work, but I just couldn't help myself. Justin's job was dangerous and he needed to be on top of his game whenever he was on the schedule.

Throughout the night, I kept dozing off and waking back up not being able to sleep because I was worried about what he was doing. I even tried calling him a few times, but he never answered any of my calls. As a result, I cried damn near the whole time as I laid in bed watching the clock, waiting to see what time he would get home.

When I heard the garage door opening then him coming up the stairs, I really tried hard to pretend like I was asleep. But when he came tiptoeing into the bedroom, making a beeline for the bathroom, I had to say something.

"So, that's what we doing now? Staying out all night has been a habit for you I see. Where in the fuck have you been all night

Justin?!" I roared as my entire body started to shake because I was so upset.

"The fuck! You scared the shit out of me. I thought you were asleep," Justin replied as he walked into the bathroom then started stripping out of his clothes.

Jumping in the shower, he proceeded to bathe as I stood there waiting for him to answer my question. After a few minutes passed of him blatantly ignoring me, I snapped out.

"So you just gone act like you didn't hear my question?"

"Ava please, don't start. All I'm trying to do is get dressed and ready for work in peace."

"Peace?! Fuck yo peace nigga! Where THE FUCK were you all night?"

"At one of my boy's house," he responded with an attitude.

"Who? Which boy?" I asked.

"Why does that even matter?"

"Which one of your boys, Justin?"

"Frank, why?"

"Hurry yo ass up in that shower cause when you get out, I want you to call Frank and prove to me that's where you were all fucking night."

"I will do no fucking such thing. Are you fucking crazy woman? It's three in the damn morning and you talking about calling somebody to prove some shit to you. You need to chill the fuck out!"

"Nah nigga you need to chill. You think I'm a fool J. Ain't no way in hell you been sitting up with a hard leg all damn night long."

"The fuck are you talking about Ava! I swear all the insecurity shit you on is a bad look for you ma. Ain't nobody said I was sitting up with him all night. Hell, I was tired than a motherfucker and ended up falling asleep. I didn't plan on staying gone as long as I did, but shit, it is what it is now."

"It is what it is huh!? Wow! Why get married if you feel like you can come and go as you please?"

"I'm a grown ass motherfucking man got damnit!" Justin yelled as he stepped out of the shower and into my face, water running down his body and all. The floor was slippery and he slightly slid into me because he was moving so fast.

"Why'd you get married Justin if you feel like this?!"

"Shit, you got me questioning that shit to death right now. I knew you were insecure, but damn I thought we were past you feeling like that. You wanted me to settle down and do right by us, so I married your ass. Took you on a honeymoon and even took an extra week off of work just to be with yo ass!" he snapped, pointing on my forehead with his forefinger as he yelled. "And that's still not good enough motherfucka!"

"Don't fuckin' touch me like that!" I scoffed, slapping his hand away from my face. "I didn't make you do shit. You were the one that claimed you wanted to fight for our relationship and proposed to me! I didn't make you do shit."

"Shit I can't tell. I did what I felt I needed to do to get you back. Had I known that once we got married, I was going to have to give my entire life up and make every fucking thing about yo ass, I would have thought twice about getting married. Now, move the fuck out of my face so I can get ready for work."

"Fuck you Justin!"

"Back at you babe. You're a real piece of work. The last thing I need is to be going into work with my energy off. Yo ass just won't let the fuck up."

"You a piece of work too nigga! You not wanting to call Frank says all that I need to know."

"What you saying got damnit?!"

"That you weren't with no hard leg. You were with a bitch!"

"Wasn't nobody with a female. I swear you should go see a counselor for your issues cause they really a bad look for you, ma."

Getting dressed in record time, he grabbed his wallet, cellphone and keys and stormed out of the bedroom, slamming to door so hard that it popped back open.

I was so upset that I couldn't even follow him. The things that had come flying out of his mouth had me fucked all the way up. The way that my mouth had hit the floor by him saying the things we had said had me stuck. Just from him being super defensive had me on guard. I had called him a couple of times last night, but his phone kept going straight to voicemail, and he never called me back once. He didn't even bother texting me to let me know that he was okay. Justin was full of shit.

Making it to the bathroom, I saw that Justin left his dirty clothes on the bathroom floor, so I picked them up and threw them in the clothes hamper. Seeing that the hamper was full, I took it out of the bathroom so that I could carry it to the laundry room. I had at least two hours before I needed to leave for work and I needed to calm my nerves because I was on ten. So I decided to get a head start on the laundry and wash a load before leaving out for work.

I carried the laundry basket to the laundry room then took the clothes that I had on off to add them to the load. Since there were a ton of dark colored clothes, I figured I'd start with them. As I was sorting out the clothes, checking them to make sure there wasn't anything in any of the pockets that would mess up my brand new Samsung washer machine, I came to the jogging pants that Justin had on when he left last night. As I went through his pockets, I found a Magnum wrapper. Annnnnd, not only was the wrapper torn open, but it was empty!

That sorry son of a bitch! I knew it! I knew his sorry monkey ass had been up to no good, talkin' about he was at his friend Frank's house. Frank's house my big ass!

Instantly, I felt sick to my stomach. I couldn't do anything but cry. I knew it. I knew that I had been feeling a type of way for a reason. My gut never steered me wrong ever! Instead of putting the clothes in the washing machine, I went back into the bedroom and grabbed my phone so that I could call Justin. Just as before, his phone went straight to voicemail. Since he wasn't answering my phone calls, I decided to take a picture of the condom wrapper and send it to him in a text with a message that read; **you one sorry, lying ass son of a bitch!**

I was so distraught and upset, all I could do was drop to the floor and weep. I couldn't show up to his job and risk getting arrested.

And I couldn't go off on him because he wasn't answering my calls, so all I could do was cry out of anger, frustration and hurt. I couldn't believe that Justin would be so malicious and step out on our marriage like that. Then just like a man, he didn't even make sure to dot his I's and cross his T's to ensure that he wouldn't get caught. Coming up in our home with a used condom wrapper in his pockets... what a disgrace!

It didn't even matter that he was smart enough to use a condom. Just the fact that he felt he had to lie to my face and lay up with another woman was so disrespectful and fucked up on his part. I knew I was feeling that he was being distant with me for a reason. I just freaking knew it! I couldn't believe that my husband had stormed out of the house yesterday talking about he needed some space just so that he could go and fuck on some bitch.

After I sat around for an hour feeling sorry for myself, my alarm clock on my cellphone went off just as it did every day at five, so that I could get up to get ready for work. Figuring I didn't have much time to continue to wallow over Justin and his shady ass, I went into the bathroom and stepped into the shower. After showering and getting dressed, I grabbed my cellphone to see if he texted me back and of course, he didn't.

I knew that once he saw the condom wrapper in my message, it would prompt his ass to call me, but he didn't. That was probably because he knew his ass was wrong and didn't want to hear what I had to say about it.

Leaving out and heading to work, I wasn't up for calling and talking to Dawn this morning. I hoped she enjoyed her date with Tate, but I really didn't want to hear about the fun she had last night when I was home alone crying like a fool while my husband was out cheating on me. Same with Shane. When we talked yesterday, he mentioned that he was expecting company. I wasn't up to hear his jovial ass brag about getting dicked down when my ass was feeling like shit. Instead of calling either one of them, I chose to drive to work in silence with nothing but my thoughts running rampant through my head.

Making it to work, I headed for the entrance and just like clockwork, Kevin opened the door and held it for me.

"Good morning Ava."

"Hey Kevin."

"You okay?"

"Yeah, I'm fine," I replied keeping it very short.

To say that I was feeling emotional would be an understatement, but I had to keep my emotions in check as best as I could. I couldn't get to my office fast enough. Closing my office door then plopping down in my chair at my desk, I instantly broke down crying. I was feeling a mixture of disappointment, anger, hurt and embarrassment all at once and was having a hard time containing it. I didn't know why I was feeling embarrassed, I guess it was because I felt like a fool. In that moment, I started to question everything; my marriage, me. Like why was I not enough for my husband?

Taking a Kleenex out of the box on my desk, I wiped the tears from my eyes and face then grabbed my makeup bag that I carried in my purse. Taking out my compact and looking in the mirror, I saw that my eyes were red and puffy, and my face looked flushed. Applying a little powder foundation to my face and Visine in my eyes, I tried my best to mask how I was feeling. Just as I was putting on some lip gloss, there was a knock on my office door.

"Just a second!" I hollered out, wondering who it could be because I wasn't due to see my first student until after second period.

Before I could reach the door to open it, the door opened and Kevin walked in. Closing the door behind him, he looked into my eyes with a concerned look on his face.

"I hate to be intrusive, but I had to come see if you were okay. You look like you had a rough night and not in a good way. Is everything okay?"

Taking a deep breath, I hesitated before I said anything. I knew that it was inappropriate for me to be talking to Kevin, especially about my personal life but fuck it. I had so much on my mind, and I knew that at the moment, I didn't want to hear what my sister or Shane had to say. Especially since before Justin and I got married, they both kept asking me if I was sure that I wanted to get married after everything that me and Justin had been through.

Then with them both feeling like I was basically being extra, I really wasn't up for talking to either one of them at the moment. I kept convincing them that things were never better between Justin and I and went ahead and married his ass when I knew I shouldn't have. Now look at me, feeling like shit cause he had been out all night with another woman. Who was to say that he was really with Tate last week when he was out and coming in late as hell?

"Ava, what's going on? I know we usually don't talk about anything personal, but you do know that you can talk to me about anything. I promise this is a no judgement zone."

Walking back to my desk, I sat back down in my office chair, dropped my head in my hands and started crying. I couldn't help the feelings that were coursing through me and when I tried to open my mouth to speak, it was like my emotions were welled up in my chest and just poured out in tears. Ugh! I hated feeling like this.

"Oh my, what happened beautiful? I'm not trying to pry into your business or upset you. I'm just concerned about you. I've never seen you upset like this before. I could tell something was up from the moment I looked into your face this morning," Kevin said as he walked over to where I was sitting.

Taking a seat on the edge of my desk, he started rubbing my back. Handing me a Kleenex from the box on my desk, he sat there rubbing my back while I got myself together. Looking into my purse, I pulled out the used condom wrapper that I found this morning and sat it on my desk.

"What's this?" Kevin asked with a confused look on his face.

"I found that this morning in my husband's pants pocket."

"Whoa! Damn!"

"Right! The ink on our marriage certificate ain't even dry yet and he's out there cheating on me. Like what the fuck! Why am I not good enough for him?!" I cried out.

"Don't say that Ava. You are good enough. It just looks like your husband doesn't appreciate nor value what he has in you."

"I knew something was off between us. My intuition is something serious. But he made me feel like I was nagging him, crowding and smothering him is what he called it. And my sister and best friend told me that I was basically just tripping, but I know my husband. We went from not being able to keep our hands off of each other to him going out and coming in late, consistently. It's like his pattern just switched up as soon as I came back to work and wasn't home to monitor his ass."

"I'm so sorry you have to go through this, sweetie."

"It's only been a week! One fucking week since we both been back to work since our honeymoon and now this!"

"Maybe you should take today off. I mean, you're dealing with a lot. Then to have to put on a brave face and deal with these crazy ass kids all day might be a bit much for you right now."

"No, I can't take today off. I have a full schedule today. I can't let these babies down because of my stupid ass husband. It's not their fault I married a sorry sack of shit for a husband."

"I get that and it's very admirable how devoted you are to your job. But sweetie, if you ain't good how you gone be there for these kids?"

"I just need a few minutes to get myself together and I'll be fine," I replied as I applied more foundation to my face, doing my best to get myself together. "I feel bad for even telling you this. I'm sorry to be putting you all in my business like this."

"Why you feel bad when I came to you and asked what was up? I've been knowing you for some years Ava. I could tell something was wrong. You shouldn't feel bad at all."

"I bet I look like an idiot right now. Ugh! How could I be so darn stupid!"

"Hey, stop all of that," Kevin comforted then continued. "You don't look stupid at all. You're upset and I don't blame you. You have every right to be pissed."

"Ha, thanks for being on my side. I wish I could say the same thing for my sister and best friend."

"So what did your husband have to say when you confronted him?"

"Ha, that's just the thing I haven't talked to him yet, at least not about the condom. Ugh! Here I go looking dumb as shit with what I'm about to say, but he didn't even come home last night. When he got in at three this morning, I confronted him for staying out all night and we got into it bad. He basically got defensive and made me feel like I was out of line for questioning him about not coming home. I didn't know about the condom until after he left. I tried calling him but of course, he didn't answer so I texted him a picture of the condom wrapper. He never replied to my message, more than likely because he knows he fucked up!" I ranted as I checked my phone for what seemed like the hundredth time to see if Justin responded to my message or tried calling me back.

"Wow! Can I make a suggestion?"

"Sure."

"I don't even know dude, but we both can agree that he knows you know he has been up to no good. Us men don't like to be questioned or confronted, whether we're right or wrong. That's why you got the defensive attitude. He basically attempted to flip the shit and make you feel bad when he knows he is the one that is wrong."

"That's exactly what happened. I'm so upset!"

"As you should be. But now that you know what's really going on, you need to figure out how you plan on moving forward with him. You are a beautiful woman. I know you know I feel that way because I have damn near complimented you every day since we started working together. Once you told me that you were married, I put all the compliments that I used to give you on ice out of respect for your marriage. But on some real shit, you too smart and beautiful to deal with a man that don't respect you."

"I hear what you're saying and thank you for the compliment, but I'm still married. It's not like he and I are just dating. I feel stuck as shit! Like I can't just walk away and end things with the snap of my fingers like that."

"Why can't you? Being married isn't a death wish sweetie."

"I didn't get married to get a divorce in less than a year though."

"Shit who does?! But if you're not being respected, being married doesn't mean you have to sit back and take shit either," Kevin said.

"So, what should I do then? Cause confronting him and trying to get the truth out of him will be a waste of my time."

"Shit, didn't you say he stayed out all night? Give his ass a taste of his own medicine."

"So, you're suggesting that I hook up with someone, have sex and stay out all night because that's what he did to me."

"I didn't say all of that. But if that's what you want to do, who am I to judge you? You can stay out all night and it not be because you hooking up with a man. You gotta be creative. You gotta switch shit up and flip that energy back on his ass. Hell, do you and act unfazed."

"You can't be serious. My HUSBAND done cheated on me and you think I should sit back and act like I'm not fazed. That's ridiculous! Hell, I can't promise that you will even see me after today cause I want to go home and grab the biggest knife in my kitchen and-"

"Whoa, whoa!" Kevin interrupted. "That's the last thing you need to do sweetie. Please don't go and do something that you will regret later. If that man can't respect you and realize how special a woman you are, he isn't worth your freedom. Look, I grew up watching my dad cheat and do my mom wrong as hell when she was the sweetest woman I have ever known. She catered to my dad's every want and need and he still went out in the streets and did him. Whenever she would confront him, things would go bad and fast. But then one day, she switched it up and didn't give him the reaction that he was expecting and my dad didn't know how to handle that. Eventually, my mom left him. When I got older and bigger in size, I asked my old man why did he used to treat my mom the way he did. Do you what he told me?"

"Let me guess, he told you to stay in a child's place and mind your business?"

"Not quite." Kevin laughed the continued "He told me that he took for granted the fact that he thought my mom would always be there and never leave him."

"Well, I guess she showed him."

"Boy did she do that. To this day, and they have been divorced over twenty years, he still tries to get my mom to let him take her out."

"Oh wow!" I chuckled for the first time today. "I don't know if I can be that strong."

"Of course you can. I don't know your husband, but I'm a man and I know that if I fucked up royally like he did and my wife, if I had one, but I don't but I'm just saying," he clarified then continued causing me to giggle. "If I knew my wife had caught my ass and didn't react and snap out on me, I wouldn't know how to handle that. Put that nigga on ice. If you feel like you can't do that in his presence, go home and get an overnight bag, grab you some clothes for the next couple of days and leave for a few days."

"Hmmmm, I don't know. I don't know how I feel about telling my sister or best friend about this just yet. And if I leave, it would have to be to one of their houses."

"Why not?"

"Because I'm not ready to hear the, I told you so's they gone say."

"How do you know they will say that?" Kevin asked.

"Because this isn't the first time that I've suspected that Justin stepped out on me. I just never caught him. He'd always say he was at his boy's house and every time I'd check, that was exactly where he was. Then like a dumbass, I went and married him. Ugh! I feel like such a fool."

"For starters, you gotta stop putting yourself down. You're not a dumbass nor are you a fool. You're just in love with a man that doesn't know your worth, love. You know us fellas always stick up for one another. You sure his friend wasn't covering for him?"

"I'm positive because I used to drive pass his friend's house and Justin's car would always be parked in his driveway. A few times, I even sat parked a few houses away from his friend's house, just to see if Justin just parked his car there and had some wanch pick him up from his friend's house. But that wasn't the case."

"So, how often and for how long would he be over there?"

"Literally all damn day and in some cases all night."

"You sure he ain't fuckin' on his friend?"

"What?!" I asked, whipping my head to the side. "That's the last thing I'm concerned about. Justin and Tate are manly men. They both think they're players and every woman wants them, if anything."

"I just had to ask cause you never know. But, if you want, I'll pay for you to stay a few nights at the Hilton by the mall. That way you can take some time to clear your mind and decide how to proceed with things. You'd be killing two birds with one stone cause I promise you, dude will be home every night that you are gone feeling the way he made you feel when he didn't come home. Trust, I know cause I'm a man."

"So, you are familiar with doing women wrong and have gotten some payback huh?"

"I mean, in my younger years, I was a motherfuckin' playa playa. I'm much more mature now and thankfully, got all of that out of my system. I ain't that dude no more. So, what do you say? I can call and reserve the room for you now if you want."

"Oh no, I wouldn't dare ask that of you. I'll figure this out."

"How about you think about it and I'll check in on you throughout the day to see how you're holding up."

"Thanks Kevin. I truly appreciate you for taking the time to talk to me. And I'll think about what you said. I feel much better than I did when I first got here if nothing else. You made some very good points and gave me a lot to think about. Thanks so much for that."

"No thanks needed friend. Try to hang in there, love. Everything will be okay and work out. I know it doesn't seem like it right now, but once you calm down and think this shit through, you'll figure things out. I'm sure of it."

"Thank for the encouragement, really. I truly appreciate it. I actually feel much better."

"Good! Mission accomplished then." Kevin laughed.

After giving me a hug, Kevin left so that I could get ready for my first meeting of the day. We had spent the whole first period talking and he truly helped me feel better. I couldn't help but to think he was right, I mean, he was a man so if anybody knew how men thought it would be him. Checking my schedule as I waited for Gwen, the student I was scheduled to see, to make it to my office, I noticed that my last two slots for the day were now open. Going into the system and checking the attendance records, I saw that by a stroke of luck the last two students I was scheduled to see didn't come to school today.

Pulling up my email, I sent one to my boss asking if I could leave after my last appointment for the day for personal reasons. Just as I hit send on my message, there was a soft knock on my office door letting me know that it was time for me to shake off my feelings and get my day started. The faster I'd get started. the quicker the day would go.

Chapter Six

Justin

When I left last night, I never expected to stay out as late as I did. After having sex, ordering in dinner then passing out and falling asleep, I never expected to stay asleep as long as I did. Thankfully, when I made it in the house Ava was still asleep or so I thought.

Calling myself tiptoeing, trying to make it to the bathroom so that I could hop in the shower, all of a sudden Ava perked up and jumped out of bed, startling the shit of out of me.

"So that's what we doing now?" Ava asked as I blew out a long exasperated breath.

She was yelling all extra loud as I did my best to tune her ass out.

"The fuck! You scared the shit out of me. I thought you were asleep," I replied as I walked into the bathroom and started stripping out of my clothes.

Getting into the shower, I did my best to ignore Ava as much as I could. But in true Ava fashion, she not only followed me into the bathroom but she continued to go off on me yelling louder and louder. She was really testing my patience. As she stood in the bathroom going off, I couldn't get my body to move fast enough so that I could finish up and leave before she pushed me to say some shit that would really hurt her feelings.

She kept trying to find out where I was last night, but if she knew what I knew she would let dead dogs lie in that case cause she wouldn't be able to handle knowing where I was and who I was with. Then when I didn't respond to her, it must have really struck one of her nerves because she then started screaming at the top of her lungs.

"Ava please, don't start. All I'm trying to do is get dressed and ready for work in peace!" I all but pleaded, hoping she would just drop the shit and leave me be.

She was acting like this was the first time that I had ever stayed out late. I was so confused why today of all days when I was trying to get in and out the house to get to work on time that she'd choose to fuck with me about some shit that done already happened.

"Peace?! Fuck yo peace nigga! Where THE FUCK were you all night?"

Now she was getting beside herself talking to me like I was some kind of pussy or something, cursing at me and all. Not once had I called her out her name, out loud at least for her to have been standing there doing all that she was doing.

I told her that I was at Frank's house, one of my friends and you'd think that she would've put a lid on her mouth and leave me be, but that wasn't good enough. She had the damn audacity to ask me to call up my boy to prove to her that I was really at her house. She really was doing the absolute most expecting me to involve people in our private matters. I wasn't like her, who ran off and told anybody willing to sit and listen to her cry them a river about me. I kept what went on in our relationship between us.

Now when she started talking about I wasn't sitting up with a hard leg all night, I instantly knew where the conversation was going to go. She was insinuating that I was with another woman when the truth I really was with a hard leg. I was with an 8 ½ hard dick, sucking and fucking the night away, but that was some information she for sure couldn't handle.

You'd think she'd just leave shit alone. That was one of the things that confused me about Ava. She knew good and damn well that she really couldn't handle the truth, so my thing was why even ask. Her shit was blowing me.

We continued to argue then one thing led to another and I flashed out on her ass. I brought up how she was insecure and she threw in my face why did I marry her. She was talking mad shit with deep bass in her voice like she was bout it, so I got bout it right along with her.

"I'm a grown ass motherfucking man got damnit!" I yelled as I stepped out of the shower and into her face. I wanted to knock the shit out of her ass because I was dripping wet and damn near fucked around and slipped and fell.

"Why'd you get married Justin if you feel like this?!" she cried, but by then her cries didn't make me feel no kind of way. She had successfully pissed me the fuck off. She didn't care that I didn't feel like being bothered, so I didn't care about what came out of my mouth next.

"Shit, you got me questioning that shit to death right now. I knew you were insecure, but damn I thought we were past you feeling like that. You wanted me to settle down and do right by us, so I married your ass. Took you on a honeymoon and even took an extra week off of work just to be with yo ass!" I snapped, pointing on her forehead with my forefinger as I tried my hardest not to yoke her ass up. "And that's still not good enough motherfucka!"

At that point, I knew that if I hadn't hurried the hell up and gotten out of there, things were going to really go left and that would not have been good for her at all. I swear I tried to go on about my way, but she just wouldn't let the fuck up and the next thing I knew, she got to talking about fuck me! The fucking nerve! So I sent that shit right back at her ass.

I came in the house and didn't plan on saying shit to her. She was the one that got up acting all dramatic and crazy and shit! Fucking with me like me coming in late was a first. She really had turned me off; big time. Then as if we hadn't insulted each other enough, now that she had my attention, she wanted to get back on the whole me calling Frank thing. I was seriously questioning why I married her ass at that point. I should have just kept her ass as a girlfriend, and lived my life real talk.

"You're a real piece of work. The last thing I need is to be going into work with my energy off. Yo ass just won't let the fuck up!" I snapped as I moved throughout the room getting my clothes on as fast as I could.

"You a piece of work too nigga! You not wanting to call Frank says all that I need to know."

"What you saying got damnit?!"

"That you weren't with no hard leg. You were with a bitch!"

"Wasn't nobody with a female. I swear you should go see a counselor for your issues cause they really a bad look for you ma."

At that point, I was done because I was seconds away from telling her who I really was with and that would have been hell for the both of us. I couldn't risk being late for work.

Thankfully, by then I was dressed. All I needed to do was grab my keys, wallet and phone and I was good to go. Once I got my shit, I got the hell out of dodge, making sure to slam the door on my way out for good measure. I needed her to know that I was pissed and that stunt she had pulled was out of order.

I was about a block away from the fire station sitting at the traffic light when I saw that Ava was calling me. I knew she couldn't have been that slow to honestly think that I wanted to answer her call. As far as I was concerned, I was done arguing with her ass. Right after I sent her bat shit crazy ass to voicemail, I got a notification on my cellphone alerting me that I had gotten a text from her.

She just couldn't catch a clue to leave the shit alone, I swear. Shaking my head, I opened her message and the first thing that I saw was a screenshot of a Magnum condom wrapper. I didn't even read what she had texted me because I damn near dropped my phone from my hands.

"FUCK!" I shouted, thinking how the fuck did she find that.

Instantly, I got pissed off because the only thing that I could think was that I must have had it in one of my pockets and her insecure ass had done gone rummaging through my shit after I left this morning. She went looking for a bone and had found one, fuck! I couldn't believe that I had messed up like that. Thank God I didn't answer her call cause sweet baby Jesus, I could only imagine how she was going to come.

Hearing cars blowing their horns behind me, I realized that the traffic light had turned green. I hadn't even noticed it because I was frazzled as hell by Ava finding that condom wrapper in my pockets like that. I ended up making it to work in good time, parked and headed inside to get my day started. As soon as I clocked in, my Chief walked up to me.

"Hey Miller, thanks for coming in today. I hate to ask you this, but instead of only working half the day can you stay all day? I really need for you to stay for the whole day."

"Ummm, sure I can stay the whole day." Perfect cause I was not in a rush to go back home no time soon.

"Thanks buddy! Keep up the good work," Chief Thompson said as he patted my shoulder then walked off.

Having to stay all day was definitely not something I wanted to do being that I was supposed to be off today, but knowing that Ava had found a condom wrapper in one of my pockets, I might not even go home tonight at all.

Heading up to the kitchen to see what was on the menu for breakfast, I realized how hungry I was. Having to work a full schedule was just what I needed to get my mind off of Ava and what I was going to have to face once she and I did cross paths later today.

End of the day

I ended up getting called out to a fire thirty minutes before I was due to get off, which wound up causing me to get home even later than I would have; a blessing from above. But now as I left work to head home, just a little past nine pm, I couldn't help but to brace myself for the wrath of Ava. She hadn't reached out to me since sending me the text message with the condom wrapper and I definitely wasn't stupid enough to reach out to her, so I knew it was about to go down as soon as I walked through the door.

Making it home, I parked my truck in the garage and headed inside bracing myself for whatever nonsense she was going to be on. When I got inside though, the house was awfully quiet and I noticed that Ava hadn't cooked dinner. Well if she did, she didn't leave a plate out for me, which was a sure sign that she was still pissed and with the way she acted earlier this morning, I wasn't surprised. As I headed upstairs, I called out to her, but there was no response.

Making it to our bedroom, I saw that she wasn't in there. "Ava! Ava! AVA!" I called out again and still no response.

So, I headed back downstairs and opened the garage door and that was when I noticed that her car wasn't even parked in the garage. I was so nervous when I first got home, mentally preparing myself for her to snap out on me as soon as I hit the door that I hadn't even realized that she wasn't home. Figuring she was still feeling some type of way and was probably either at Shane's or her sister's crying them a river and telling them our business, I headed to the bathroom to take a shower.

After taking a shower then getting dressed, I went down to the kitchen to find something to eat. I started to call or text Ava to see if she wanted me to order her something for dinner, but after thinking about it, I figured she more than likely had already eaten. Knowing that she was pissed off, I was sure that this was her way of trying to get my attention. But the shit wasn't working because I really wasn't fazed by what she was doing.

I ended up ordering a meat lover's pizza from Lou Malnati's. Thankfully, it didn't take long to be delivered because I was starvin' like Marvin. After eating, I stretched out on the sofa in the family room with plans of watching a little TV but ended up dozing off to sleep.

Waking up out of my sleep, I needed to use the washroom, so I headed to the bathroom to relieve myself. Checking the time on the stove in the kitchen as I walked by on my way to the half bathroom down the hall, I saw that it was a little past one in the morning. After using the bathroom, I headed upstairs to check on Ava. I hadn't heard her when she got in and I was surprised she didn't wake me up. Making it to our bedroom, I realized why she hadn't woken me up. It was because she hadn't made it home yet.

Being that it was a weeknight and she needed to be up in the morning for work, I couldn't understand why she hadn't made it in the house yet. Heading back downstairs, I grabbed my cellphone so that I could call her to see where she was. At this point, she was taking things too far, acting childish by not coming home nor calling me or at least texting me to tell me that she wouldn't be coming home.

Going to her number in my call log, I hit send and the call went straight to voicemail. Hanging up, I tried calling her again and just as before the call went right to voicemail. Now she had me hot with her petty Betty ass. I knew she was upset about the condom wrapper, but to not come home or answer my calls was being a bit too dramatic; talk about putting a ten on a damn two! Sitting on the couch, I started to get worried that maybe something happened to her. I figured if that were the case, someone would have reached out to me by now. With me working for the fire department and Tate working as an EMT, we knew our co-workers' families very well. With EMTs working alongside of us on some calls, we all knew each other.

The only person I could think to call was her friend Shane. I didn't want to call her sister just yet because I assumed that she was one of the first people Ava called after I left this morning and I knew her sister didn't really care for me. I couldn't even blame her for not liking me because Ava stayed on her sister's main line telling her all types of fucked up shit about me with her insecure ass. I mean yes, I did have a very bad habit of cheating on my wife, but she'd accuse me of cheating on her with a woman and that wasn't the case. So, as far as I was concerned, the bullshit she told Dawn about me was just that... bullshit.

Her sister and I used to be cool, but when Ava and I went through our rough patch, she confided in Dawn. I felt like that was when Dawn's feelings for me changed. I felt like she never really liked me again after all that had gone down between us and that she was just tolerating me because Ava loved me. And, although Ava never really found out that I had cheated on her and it was proven that every time I'd leave the house and say I was at Tate's, that was exactly where I was, I was still wrong in Dawn and Ava's eyes because I still made Ava feel lonely and I'd hurt her feelings for not giving her enough attention. Obviously that was more than enough for her sister to change how she felt about me moving forward permanently.

The only other person in the world that I could think to call was Ava's best friend, Shane. I knew that Ava also told Shane EVERYTHING that had gone on in our relationship for a fact because he would always tell me whenever he and I would talk or see each other. As bad as it made me feel to admit this, Shane and I had been messing around with each other for the last couple of months. I knew it was fucked up as hell for me to be sleeping around with my wife's best friend, but he was just as wrong as I was. Hell, there were even times when I'd be at his house and he'd put his phone on speaker so that I could hear Ava crying the blues to him about me.

Going to his number in my phone that was saved under S.B., I couldn't save it under his real name because as insecure as Ava was, I didn't want to risk her ever going through my phone and seeing his name in my phone. I decided to send him a text instead of call him just in case Ava was over to his house.

Me: Hey what you doing

S.B: I'm in bed... why you wanna join me or something

Me: Is Ava at your house

S.B: Would I have asked you to come join me in bed if she was?!?!?!?

I swear Shane was a handful when he wanted to be.

Me: Obviously not. I thought you were playing around truthfully

S.B: As horny as I am right now I'm serious as a heart attack

Me: All you think about is sex

S.B: That's cause you got that good wood

Me: Have you talked to Ava today

S.B: No, I haven't actually. She's not at home?

Me: Didn't I just ask if she was at your house

S.B: So what happened this time

Me: For one she was livid when I made it home from your house this morning. You could have at least woken me up so that I could get home at a reasonable time

S.B: Aht, aht! Don't blame me for you not making curfew. I'm single and can mingle without having to answer to anybody. I ain't the one that is married booski

Me: I'm not blaming you I'm just saying. Then she ended up finding a condom wrapper in my pocket

S.B: Now see you just plain dumb!

Me: Whatever! I'll talk to you later. I need to find out where your crazy ass friend is at

S.B: Do you want me to call her

Me: Hell no! It's 1 in the morning. That's obvious as fuck. If she not with you then she's with Dawn.

S.B: Well if you get lonely, the right side of my bed and I would love the company

Me: NO! That's what got my ass in trouble in the first place. Let me get shit right with her and I'll check with you later. We can hook up then

S.B: Ok. Text me if you need me. Good luck cause you gone need it

Ugh! Since she wasn't at Shane's, that meant that she was at her sister's house. Just great, now I'ma have to more than likely have to deal with not just Ava going off on me, but her sister's ass also. I swear Ava did the damn most. All she had to do was bring her ass home and we could have had a conversation about the shit.

Shane

After Justin texted me asking if Ava was at my house or if I had talked to her, I knew then that he had fucked up royally. Justin tried me calling himself putting part of the blame on me talking about I should have woken his ass up cause he ended up oversleeping, but that was on him. Hell, I was just as tired as his ass was after we got done fucking on each other so that shit was not my fault that he overslept. I was sort of shocked about Ava snapping on him about getting home late because she usually complained to me more about it instead of addressing it with him.

That was part of the reason why Justin had a bad habit of having no issues with staying out late. Ava had created a monster and hadn't even realized it until it was too late.

When Justin and I first started fucking around, it was when he and Ava had broken up because she thought he was cheating on her with some chick. While they were broken up, Justin had come to my shop for a haircut and lining one day and somehow, one thing led to another and we ended up hooking up later that night when I got off of work. Ever since then, we had been fucking around with each other faithfully. Justin's sex game was intoxicating, I couldn't lie. I was addicted to him as much as he was addicted to me.

I was no fool because I knew that I wasn't just sharing him with Ava. To be honest, I sort of felt like since they were on break when we started our fuckship that he was stepping out on me with Ava and mainly using her as a coverup for him being bi-sexual. But, being the good friend to Ava that I was, I never acted no type of way about them getting back together. And, whenever I was around her and Justin at the same time, I always played it cool. In fact, I was very supportive of their relationship, as well as their marriage.

I knew that there was someone else in his life because Ava told me everything about her relationship with him. Sometimes, she'd be upset about Justin not coming home until late at night and he and I hadn't been together that particular today. But I wasn't really trippin' about that either because I had my share of honey dips, so it was what it was. One thing about him and I was that we didn't discuss all of our sex partners with each other.

I didn't feel that I needed to tell him my business and I wasn't interested in knowing any of his. To be honest, I really wasn't interested in knowing all that. I was privy to too much when it came to him and my bestie, but again, being the good friend that I was to Ava, I was always there for her to vent to.

As I laid in bed after texting with Justin about him and Ava falling out and her not going home, I couldn't help but to keep getting the urge to call her. Justin said for me not too because it would look too obvious and I got that. Like, how was I supposed to know that they had got into it and she hadn't come home, especially with it being after one in the morning. She never called me to tell me what had happened. So, as I laid here in bed, I tried to think of a good decoy story to come up with as my excuse for calling her.

Knowing that she was at her sister's house, in a way, I didn't want to call this late and have her smart mouthed ass sister say some slick shit. Dawn and I were cool, but it was only on the strength that she and Ava were sisters. It was no secret that we didn't care for each other... we just tolerated one another because we were civilized adults. With it being so late and knowing that they both had to be up early for work, including myself, I decided to wait until later in the morning to call Ava. In the meantime, I laid in bed and pondered over what lie I could come up with to not make myself look obvious for when I did call her. Then I dozed back off to sleep.

The Next Morning

Waking up bright and early, I reached for my phone before I had even got out of bed to brush my teeth or wash and clean my ass and face. I was super anxious to get the tea on what happened. Going to my text thread, I figured I'd hit Justin up first to see if Ava had come home before I'd reached out to her.

Me: Good moaning

Jay: What's up? Have you heard from your bestie

Me: Nope, that's why I'm checking in with you. Have you heard from her

Jay: Nope. Her ass is acting super petty. Keep me posted if she reaches out to you

Me: You know I will

Jay: Thanks

Me: I hope I get to see you later

Jay: Text me when you get off work

Me: Bet

After texting Justin, I went to my call log and scrolled to Ava's name. Pulling up her number then hitting send, I waited for her to answer the phone, but the call went straight to voicemail. Hanging up then trying to call again, the same thing happened; the call went to voicemail. Not really thinking too much about it, I got out of bed then headed into the bathroom so that I could wash my ass and get my day started. Three hours later, I was dressed, smelling divine and looking like a whole meal ready to head off to work.

I was finally cutting and lining my last client for the day and I couldn't have been any happier. My feet were killing me and I was so hungry that I could eat an ox. Once I was done with my last client, I checked my cellphone to see if I had any messages or missed calls and realized that I hadn't heard from Ava at all today either. She and I talked every day, so that was unusual for her to not call me, especially with this being two days that she and I haven't talked.

Going to her number in my log, I called her up, but the call went to voicemail. At this point, it was obvious that her ass had her phone turned off. Going to the Facebook app on my phone and logging in, I checked to see if she was online, but she wasn't. Digging a little deeper, I went to my Facebook messenger to see if it showed when the last time was that she was online and it didn't even have a time. Ava was clearly beside herself and now, I was starting to worry hoping that she hadn't done anything crazy because she was M.I.A.

I stopped at the grocery store Jewel to get some crab legs, shrimp, and andouille sausage so that I could cook up a quick crab boil before heading home. Making it to the house, I prepared my crab boil, popped it in the oven then jumped in the shower so that I could change into something comfortable. Once I was done, I decided to give Justin a call to see if he had an update on Ava's whereabouts and to see if he was still planning on coming over.

"Hey boo, any update on my bestie?"

"Nope, every time I call, her phone goes to voicemail."

"Same here. I know you said not to call her, but it's not like her to not call me at least once a day. I haven't heard from her in two days. I sure hope that she is okay."

"Her ass is fine she's just acting out. I thought about calling Dawn, but I don't want to have to deal with her ass."

"Lord, this isn't like her to just up and disappear though."

"I noticed that one of her overnight bags is gone, so I know she is good and that she planned this lil disappearing act she done pulled."

"Well, just give her some time to get out of her feelings. She'll be back. I'm just shocked that she's that pissed about you coming in late. Like, she hasn't tripped out like this before about that. What made this time so different?"

"My thoughts exactly. But she went rummaging through the clothes I had on that night and found a condom wrapper."

"Whoa!" I interrupted. "How could you be so careless fool!"

"Man look, I forgot about the damn wrapper to be honest. I didn't think she would go looking through my shit I guess."

"Men can be so slow. Come on now! You gotta do better Justin. Woman are master investigators. If they wanna find some shit out that's just what they gonna do. I thought you were smarter than that. Hell, I wouldn't be surprised if she hasn't smelled your drawers a time or two,"

"Smelled my drawers! What the fuck yo! That's some nasty shit. Ava told you she smelled my fuckin' drawers before?"

"Oh no love, that's something she probably wouldn't tell a sole if she has done it before. I'm just saying, you need to be way more careful. No wonder she up and ghosted on yo ass."

"Well, for what's it's worth she should have been more concerned with getting ready for work and not rummaging through my clothes in my opinion. I was always told if you go looking for trouble, trouble is just what you're gonna find," he said.

"True, but you're the ass that's in trouble fool, not her."

"Whatever Shane. I'm done talking about the shit. All I gotta say is that your bestie is foul for leaving and not at least checking in, but it's cool. She don't like that shit happening to her, but she turns around and does the shit to me. But it's whatever."

"On another note, I cooked some crab legs and shrimp. I just took it out the oven actually. I'll save you some if you want. Have you eaten anything today?"

"No, not since this morning. Good looking out. I'm on my way over now."

"Okay boo, see you when you get here."

Hanging up with Justin, I felt better knowing that Ava had packed her a few pieces of clothes and planned on leaving. For a minute, I was hoping nothing crazy had happened to her. Justin leaving a condom wrapper in his pocket was just plain stupid. If he didn't start being more careful, I was going to have to either ease up on him a bit before he blew our cover or school him on how to cover his tracks cause that was some bullshit.

Chapter Seven

Ava

Four Days Later

"Good morning sissy. How are you feeling this bright, beautiful morning?" Dawn answered, sounding extra chipper.

"Good morning sis! I'm actually feeling a lot better than I was yesterday. I feel way more refreshed and well rested thankfully. How are you feeling?"

"I'm good. I'm actually on time and not running late this morning. Can you believe it?!" She giggled then continued. "You still planning on going back home today?"

"Oh my! You're not running late! That's a first," I cheered. "Yes, I think I have taken enough days to myself to think things through."

"So, do you know what you're going to do about your cheating ass husband?"

"Well dang sis, how do you really feel!?"

"Trust me, you don't want to know the answer to that," Dawn emphasized sarcastically.

"You're probably right." I giggled. "To be honest, I know what my gut is telling me to do, but I haven't made any final decisions yet."

"I hope it's telling you that you deserve better and that you need to leave Justin's cheating ass the fuck alone."

"I know I deserve better. I just want to hear him out. I want to know what drove him to cheat on me like that."

"Why?! Does it really matter? Like, will it change anything about how he made you feel or what he did? At the end of the day, if you want to know why he cheated, I can answer that... his ass is selfish as fuck! That's why."

"Well gosh! Aren't you fired up and full of energy and honesty this morning?"

"I'm not trying to be too harsh, but I love you sissy. I hate it when you're upset, especially over a no- good ass man who doesn't know what he has at home. That shit is played out and not cool at all. I get that you love Justin and all, but something's gotta give.

Finding a condom wrapper, and a used one at that, in his pocket after he had been out all night is all the proof you need that his ass doesn't respect y'all's marriage. What does it matter what he has to say? Hell, what are you really looking for him to say exactly... sorry? Cause sorry ain't gone change nor fix the damage that's already done sis."

"I know and you're right, but Justin and I are married now, not just dating. Everything that you're saying is absolutely true, but you're speaking from the mind frame of a single woman. You're not thinking like a married woman. I just feel that at the very least, he owes me some kind of explanation. It's hard for me to just be done and say fuck it all like you can. You wouldn't understand because you're a hard ass, but I'm not like that."

"I don't think the fact that I'm not married matters 'cause I'd still feel the same way. Married or not, if my dude cheats and I catch his ass it's a wrap. I'ma cancel that fool then keep it moving."

"Lawd Dawn, I swear."

"I'm just saying. I just hope you don't fall for the oh-kee-doke and choose to stay with his ass. You don't deserve to be treated like that sissy and that's all I'm trying to say. You deserve to be with a man that knows your worth. Not a fool that can't appreciate you."

"Thanks sissy, I appreciate that. All I ask is that you be patient with me. I trust and confide in you because I need someone to talk to. Me confiding in you isn't for you to turn against Justin and be ready for war. I'm a big girl and I'll figure this all out. I just be needing someone to vent to someone is all," I explained.

"You don't have to worry about turning me against Justin because I never liked his ass anyway. As far as being ready for war, I stay on go when it comes to those I love. Sorry sis, that ain't gone change. I know you'll figure things out and either way I'ma have your back, but at some point, you gone has to realize that a zebra can't change his stripes."

"Oh my God, Dawn! Stop it! Lawd, I was feeling all relaxed and now you got my nerves hot. I get what you're saying, but now you got me feeling some type of way and that's not why I called."

"Okay, okay, but for real. Have you talked to Shane about what happened?"

"No, I've only talked to you about it."

"WHAT! You mean to tell me you didn't tell girlfriend what happened?"

"Now you know you wrong calling my bestie "girlfriend". No, I haven't talked to him. I tried calling him last night, but he didn't answer. Okay so, enough about me, how are you and Tate?"

"Tate and I are good. He is a really sweet guy-"

"Ah shit, I know where this is about to go!" I interrupted, "When you start off saying a guy is sweet, that means you done friend zoned his ass."

"Ha! You know me so well!" Dawn laughed. "There is just something about him that I can't quite put my finger on."

"Why you say that sis? I swear you always trying to analyze people. Have you ever tried going with the flow and just accepting people for who they are, without having to question everything?"

"Girl no, have you?" Dawn chuckled.

"Well yes, I take people for who they are."

"And no offense but look where that shit done got you!"

"Ouch! That was harsh Dawn, really!" I said.

"Harsh and honest sissy."

"Ugh! Yo ass is so aggy! How do you expect to ever fall in love and get married if you're always so critical about everyone and everything?"

"For one, who said anything about me wanting to get married? I plan to be single and mingle for as long as possible chile. I can't be tied down to one man. It's way too many for the picking. Then to pour my all into someone for them to turn around and hurt me… girl, I'm straight on that. I'd fuck around and catch a *Snapped* case on some real-life shit."

"Oh my God sis! You're too much!" I busted out laughing. "Well, I just made it to work. I'll call you later and update you on how everything goes."

"Okay, sissy! Love you and have a good day. Oh, and if that fool cut up, call me asap cause I'm bout sick of his ass."

"Bye fool! Love you too."

Hanging up with Dawn, I couldn't help but to laugh to myself at our conversation. She was one of the most critical people that I knew. Although everything that she had said was a thousand percent true, I still couldn't help but to feel annoyed because I was tired of constantly hearing what's wrong with Justin as if I didn't know already. Dawn and I were polar opposites. I'd just have to take what she says with a grain of salt to not get offended cause she was straight up no chaser when it came to telling it like it was. Gathering my things then getting out of the car, I headed to the front entrance so that I could get my day started.

"Good morning Ava! Don't you look amazing this beautiful Thursday morning."

"Thanks Kevin, good morning to you as well. I actually feel amazing today. I was finally able to get some good sleep last night."

"That's a blessing. I'm glad you're feeling better."

"Me too. Thanks again for looking out for me. I truly appreciate that. I'll pay you back for the hotel room you got for me tomorrow when we get paid," I said.

"Now I done already told you not to worry about it. You don't have to pay me back for anything, it was no biggie."

"I know, but you didn't have to do that."

"I know I didn't, but I wanted to. Now, if you insist on repaying me, how bout we do lunch or dinner... when you're available of course. No pressure," he said as he raised his hands in the air.

"Okay, gotchu." I giggled. "I checked out of the room this morning, by the way."

Kevin had insisted on putting the charges for the room I got at the Hilton on his credit card. When I checked in on Monday, he told me to stay for as long as I needed. I figured four days was plenty. I didn't want to continue to rack up a bill on his card by staying any longer, so I checked out of the room before I came to work. I would have loved to stay longer, but I really needed to get back home and address with my husband about what he had done.

"Oh yeah, so you're going back to the house huh? Are you ready for that?"

"I think that I am. Justin and I need to talk and the sooner I can get this talk over with the better."

"I can understand that. Well, if you need anything or need to talk, I'm ya boy."

"Thanks Kevin, I appreciate you. Thanks so much for being such a sweet friend."

Heading inside with a big smile on my face, I figured I should relish in the moment because later on today I had a feeling I wasn't going to be smiling. I hadn't been home since Monday morning and I hadn't talked to Justin since we got into it, so I knew Justin was going to be pissed off, but I honestly didn't give a damn. For the first few days, I had my phone on Do Not Disturb so that I could be to myself. The only person that I had spoken to was Dawn and that was because I wanted to give her a heads' up about where I was in case Justin were to call her looking for me.

I didn't tell Shane what was going on because I didn't have to worry about Justin reaching out to him. I knew that Justin didn't particularly care for Shane, so that was the least of my worries.

The first couple of nights that I was gone, I didn't feel like being bothered with anyone. But last night, I wanted to check in with Shane. I just couldn't get ahold of him. I figured tonight would be a good night to go back to the house because Justin worked Friday and Saturday, so I guess we'd talk tonight then I'd have the next two days to myself to figure out what my next move would be.

It was clear that Dawn wanted me to leave Justin, and in a way that was probably not a bad idea and for the best, but I loved my husband. I wanted to hear him out at the very least. I needed to know why he felt the need to be with another woman and why he felt that I wasn't enough for him. I wanted to know where I was lacking in our relationship because I truly thought that things were going good with us.

As long as we'd been together and as much as we had gone through, I felt that I wasn't wrong for feeling that way. I got what Dawn was saying that it wouldn't change what happened, but she didn't understand what it was like to be in love and married, giving your all to a man and damn near loving him more than I loved myself. I needed an explanation or to see if he would be honest with me, so that I could have peace of mind with moving on. Making it to my office, I settled in ready for the day ahead.

"Knock, knock..." Kevin said as he walked into my office. "I just came by to check on you before you left for the day. I wanted to see if you needed to talk before you went home and faced the devil."

"Oh wow! Not the devil, huh?" I cracked up laughing. "I'm good though. Thanks for checking in with me. I think I'm ready to hear what he has to say."

"I'm glad you took my advice and gave yourself some time to think things through. You're a very intelligent woman Ava. I admire your strength and how you're handling this whole situation."

"Aww thanks so much, Kevin. That's really sweet of you to say. I wish my sister would understand as much as you do."

"Cut her some slack. I'm sure your sister loves you and just wants the best for you just as I do. Seriously, I mean that. I ain't gone lie though. I was pretty concerned about you on Monday. You were pretty hurt and upset, but seeing you hold your head up high and do what you needed to do for YOU over the past couple of days was pretty sexy to watch."

"It wasn't easy, and my feelings are still pretty hurt, but I'm much better than I was on Monday."

"How bout you take my number and if things don't go as planned tonight, or if you need anything, you can give me a call. I'll make sure to be on stand-by."

"Oh, I don't know Kevin... I'm still married and-"

"And what? You're acting like I just asked you to be my lady or some shit. It's strictly platonic. I know you're still married and I'm not trying to interfere with your marriage. I'm just trying to be your friend and be there for you is all," Kevin responded as he wrote his number down on a sticky note that was on my desk. "I'll leave the ball in your court. If you want to use my number feel free. If not, no hard feelings."

"Okay I hear you. Thanks again for everything Kevin."

After Kevin left my office, I saved his number in my phone then gathered my things so that I could head home. Now that I was going home, I couldn't lie, my nerves were getting the best of me. I didn't know why I was so nervous to go home and talk to Justin, but I knew that I needed to get it over with. Plus, I was anxious to see what he had to say for himself.

Making it to my car, I headed to the house. On my way there, I figured I'd try to call Shane just to take my mind off of things for bit, so that I could calm my nerves and keep a leveled head.

"Well, well, well! Chhhhhhiiiillllleeee! Where in the hell have you been! I was about to put a damn BOLO out on ya ass girl!" Shane said, answering the phone in true Shane fashion.

"Bestie you know your ass is crazy!"

"No seriously sweetie, where the hell have you been gurl? I have been calling and calling you and your phone was going straight to voicemail. Shit, you had me over here worried shitless about yo ass. What's been going on with you chile?"

"It's a long ass story."

"Well hell, I ain't got nothing but time. What's going on?"

"I found out that Justin has been cheating on me."

"Girl WHAT!? Say it ain't so! What done happened nah?" Shane interrupted sounding shocked as hell.

"He stayed out all night and when he got in Monday morning, we got into it. When he left, since I was up early and had a little time to spare, I decided to do a load of clothes. When I checked his pockets before putting his pants in the washer, I found a used condom wrapper."

"Well, at least his ass had enough sense to wear a condom."

"Really Shane!"

"I'm just sayin' chile."

"That still doesn't take away from the fact that he cheated on me."

"Girl I know and that is some fucked up shit. Wow! I'm so sorry bestie."

"Thanks bestie."

"So, what did he have to say for himself?" Shane asked.

"We haven't talked since Monday morning."

"So, you just been walking around his ass not talking about the shit chile? Giiiiirrrrrlll, you betta than me cause I would have been snapped out on his ass."

"That's the thing, I haven't been home. I ended up getting a room at the Hilton for a few nights. I just checked out this morning. I needed to get my mind right and knew that had I gone home, all we would have done was argue and fight," I explained.

"Why didn't you call me girl? You know you could have come over here. You didn't need to spend any money on no room at the Hilton when I have a spare room here."

"I know and thanks for that, but I needed to be alone to think things through. Now I need to figure out what to do."

"So, you thinking about leaving him for good or do you think y'all can work things out?" Shane questioned.

"To be honest, I don't even know friend. I guess that just depends on how things go tonight. If I leave it up to Dawn, I'd be filing for divorce."

"Girl bye, that's why her ass ain't got no man. I get that's your sister and all, but her ass can be negative as hell sometimes. Like, you need to do what you feel is best for you. Just know I have your back no matter what you decide booski. I hope you know that."

"I know and that's why I love you. Welp, I'm pulling into the garage now. I'll keep you posted on how things go," I said.

"Okay girl! Take you a few moments before you go inside then let his ass have it chile!" Shane laughed.

"Okay bestie, love you."

"Love you too boo."

Listening to Shane's advice, I sat in the car for a couple of minutes. What I loved about Shane was the fact that he wasn't super critical about anything I shared with him. I was able to talk him without having to feel judged or made to feel bad about what I was going through. I appreciated that the most about him. He was a really good friend.

As I sat in my car, I knew that Justin was at home because his car was parked in the garage. Taking a deep breath then exhaling, I got out of my car and headed inside the house. I could have sworn that I heard a dog barking. Opening the door to the garage and walking into the kitchen, my suspicions were correct when I saw the cutest little English bulldog puppy run up to me barking and wagging its tail.

"Oh, my goodness! Hey little puppy!" I cooed, bending down to pick the puppy up. "Aren't you just the cutest little thing ever!" I gushed.

"So, look who decided to finally come home. Where have you been Ava?" Justin asked stepping into the kitchen.

"We need to talk Justin," I replied as I put the puppy down then patted and rubbed on his stomach.

"Oh, ya think? I agree we do need to talk. Let's start with where you been for the last four days Ava!" Justin replied as he stood there watching me play with the puppy.

"I needed some time to sort things out."

"We're married. You can't just pick up and leave whenever you want to and not say anything to me about where you are! That shit wasn't cool at all."

"Oh really!" I jeered. "You got a lot of nerve. It's funny that you say that, but you think you can leave whenever the hell you want and go fuck on some trick and think the shit is okay Justin! What the fuck!" I sneered. "I want to know why? What have I done to you that was so bad for you to do me like that?"

"First off, let me explain. It's not what you think."

"Oh, save it. I found a condom wrapper in your pocket J, really! Try again cause you can't lie and get yourself out of this shit. And please don't say that you were with Tate and the condom wrapper was his cause that would be some dumb shit you'd say. At the end of the day, you cheated. So, if you're not going to come clean and dumb the shit down, then I don't want to hear shit."

"Speaking of that, you were wrong for searching through my shit! I've never gone searching through your shit! What possessed you to do that?!"

"I know you're fucking lying to me! What possessed me? For the record, I wasn't searching through your shit. I was putting a load in the washer and came across it when I checked your pockets as I always do before putting clothes in the machine, crazy ass man. And you never search through my shit because

I've never given you a reason to do no shit like that. Hell, the way I see it is we are married now and if I want to search through your shit, I fuckin' can, especially since you don't seem to have any respect for me or our marriage! Staying out all night like your ass is single."

"Yeah okay, that's your story. Like you should talk! Yo ass was just gone for four fucking days and ain't said a motherfucking thing to me about it. You just up and left like THAT shit was cool!"

"Boy bye! Cause me leaving to get peace of mind because my husband chose to step out on our marriage is no comparison to what you did!"

"Like I said, that's your story!" Justin sneered, not understanding where I was coming from.

"Really, so what's your story then? Who is this bitch that you been out fucking around on me with?"

"Look, I fucked up okay?"

"Who was it, Justin?" I asked. I didn't want to hear shit about how he fucked up. I already knew that. I just wanted to know who the hell he was fucking around with.

"Who it is doesn't matter, cause the shit didn't mean nothing. I'm sorry. I made a mistake and it will never happen again. Can we just get pass this and start over please?"

"I know you fucking lying to me! We can't just get pass shit! I want to know what made you do what you did."

"I said that I was sorry. I promise you don't have to worry about me ever doing nothing like that again."

"So, is that what the puppy is for? A sympathy gift, huh! You're really a piece of work dude."

"Now come on Ava. You said you wanted a dog, so I got you one. I just admitted to you that I was wrong, and I apologized. What's the problem now?! Like what the fuck, I can't catch a break to save my soul with yo ass!"

"What do you want me to say J? Really, how do you expect for me to feel? I have done everything in my power to show you that I love you and would do anything for you and you repay me by cheating on me! I fuck you when you want. I cook, keep a clean house and wash your damn dirty ass draws! Hell, I'm EVERY WOMAN to you and you still managed to go astray. Did you ever stop to think how I would feel? Do you feel any guilt for what you have done to our marriage... to me?"

"Look, I get it."

"I don't think you do. You think getting me a puppy is going to make what you did just disappear! Fuck you J! I can't do this anymore with you. You don't love or respect me. It's a shame that it took for me to catch your ass to finally get it. I just want to know why you married me in the first damn place! Huh, why did you fucking marry me J just to turn around and hurt me like this?" I cried. Now I was crying tears because he was talking nonsense trying to make me feel wrong for taking time for myself when he was the one in the wrong. The fucking nerve of him!

"First off, I married you because I love you Ava. Like I said, I fucked up and if you give me another chance, you'll never have to worry about me ever hurting you again. Just give me one more chance to prove to you that I want you and only you. I want our marriage and I love you... only you. I didn't mean it... I promise you I didn't. I was just pissed off when I left the other night and I did something that I shouldn't have done. I promise to you that I will never do it again. Just please forgive me this one time. Please babe," Justin said as he walked up to me and wiped the tears that had fallen from the side of my face with the back side of his hand.

"I don't know. I think we need a little time apart from each other."

"Time apart!? What do you mean we need a lil time apart? Those four days you were away wasn't enough?"

"Not by a longshot cause you don't get that what you did was wrong. All you focused on is the fact that I left to clear my mind."

"I miss you baby. PLEASE," he pleaded. "Please baby, please just give me one more chance for me to prove you're the only WOMAN, that I want and need. Baby don't throw away all we have worked so hard for over one lil mistake. I hate sleeping in an empty bed. I need you Ava."

"I don't know Justin. To me, that was a bit more than just some lil mistake. How would you feel if I would have gone out and cheated on you?"

"Babe come on now! That isn't fair."

"How would you feel Justin?" I asked needing to know the answer.

"Babe I would be pissed off. But,-"

"Aht, there's not but," I started but he interrupted me.

"There is a but damn it, let me talk!" Justin shouted. "I apologized and admitted that I was wrong. Doesn't that mean anything? How many times do I have to say that I'm sorry for you to get that I know what I did was wrong? Look, if it makes you feel any better, I'll even go to counseling. Shit, we can go together. I'll do whatever it takes to prove to you that I will never hurt you like that ever again. Babe please, I'm literally beggin' you here!"

Before I could say anything else, the puppy squatted and took a long piss right where Justin and I were standing.

"Look, I'll even clean the dog piss up even though that's your dog and your job to do."

"I'll clean the piss up myself if you think you deserve forgiveness that easily! You really just tried me."

"So, what you sayin'? You don't want to work things out with me?" he asked as he started cleaning up after the dog.

"I don't know what I want to do honestly. I just need some more time."

"What do you mean you need more time? I don't think it's healthy for our marriage to not stay in the same house and at least try."

"I never said I was leaving. We just gone have to take things day by day and see what happens. I swear to you, if you pull any more bullshit, it's a wrap."

With that, I grabbed my overnight bag then headed upstairs to our bedroom.

Chapter Eight

Justin

I couldn't believe that Ava's ass had pulled a whole disappearing act and been missing in action for days like that. I get that she was upset about the whole condom thing, but how were we going to be able to address it and move past the shit if she wasn't here? Just as I had gotten back inside the house from walking the puppy that I had gotten for Ava, I heard my cellphone ringing. Seeing that it was Shane calling, I didn't stop what I was doing to answer because I had my hands full.

Taking the leash off the dog then putting some fresh water in his bowl, I heard my phone going off again. Huffing and puffing, I went to answer it but by the time I made it to the phone Shane had hung up. I was starting to get frustrated because too much was happening all at once. I was trying to get the dog situated and Shane was blowing my damn phone up. The shit was starting to frustrate the hell out of me.

If Ava woulda brought her ass home, she could have walked and fed her own damn dog!

I really didn't want the added responsibility of taking care of a pet. The only reason why I bought it was because I wanted to extend an olive branch to my wife for fucking up and getting caught. Just as fast as Shane hung up, he called back a third time.

"Dude, what's the damn emergency?" I fumed as I watched the dog lay across the kitchen floor at my feet then turn onto his back.

"About damn time you answered! I thought you were ignoring me or something."

"My phone was charging, and I was out walking this damn dog. You know I don't keep my shit attached to my hip like you do."

"Awww, look at you being all domestic and shit."

"So, what's the emergency that got you calling me back to back and shit? You calling me like there's a damn fire."

"Nigga there is a fire! I just hung up with your wife!" he blurted then continued. "She's on her way home now. I hope you have your ass there cause from what I gathered, she's ready for war."

"She called you or you called her?"

"What does that matter. Just know she should be there any minute."

"What did she say to you?" I probed, trying to get all the information that I could so that I could mentally prepare for when Ava got home.

"Shit, she told me about what happened and all I have to say is if we're going to continue seeing each other, you gone have to do better fool. You gone fuck around and her ass gone find out about us and I don't need those types of problems."

"I know you not trying to act like us fucking around is all on me. Hell, y'all call each other besties and you fuckin' on me without a care in the world!" I snapped appalled that he had the nerve to call me talking shit.

The way I saw it, he was just as wrong for fucking around with me. Shit, I knew I was her husband, but he was supposed to be her best fucking friend!

"You the one that's married nigga!"

"Watch how you coming at me dude."

"Shit, we can call it quits and I wouldn't give a good gotdamn! I didn't even call you to get into it with your ass. I was calling to give you a heads up that she was on her way home. But if you gone be with the shits with me, fuck it! I'm out!"

"Hol' up, I didn't mean to upset you. You just be talking crazy sometimes and you know how I feel about that shit. I never said anything about us not seeing each other anymore. You said that shit. I may have slipped up once, but I'll never do anything to get us both caught up. I ain't that damn careless."

"Hell nigga, I can't tell cause yo ass is for damn sure caught up now."

"Like I said, it was one little slip up. I can assure you that it won't happen again," I said.

"Well, you need to make sure cause I ain't trying to beef with my friend over no dick. It's too many niggas out here I can fuck on than to be risking my friendship over you."

"Why you always gotta talk shit Shane?"

"Nigga I ain't talking shit. I'm speaking real facts to yo ass. Hell, you need to know where we stand cause yo ass was the one that got caught slippin', not me. So, don't be coming at me about I'm wrong about a damn thing!" Shane rambled working my nerves with his dramatic, slick talking ass.

"Okay, I hear you. Damn, my bad! Chill out, will ya. You gone catch a whole aneurysm gapping out."

"I'm just saying so we both clear."

"Thanks for giving me a heads up," I responded, not wanting to continue to go back and forth with him any longer.

"Yeah, whatever. Have you at least thought about what you going to tell her? Cause you gone have to fess up to doing wrong. I hope you know that."

"I mean, yes and no. I'ma apologize but I ain't about to tell it all."

"Boy, yo ass playing with fire!" Shane said with a laugh.

"I got this. I told you I was going to get her a puppy, so I did. That should help me smooth things out with her. Once she sees this little puppy, I'ma be back in like Flynn. Watch what I tell you. If I know anything, I know my wife. Ava pulled this little stunt for attention, but her ass ain't really trying to leave me cause if she was, she would have been left."

"Okay Mr. Arrogant, if you say so."

"What you mean, I know so!" I huffed full of pride, feeling myself because I knew Ava like I knew the back of my hand.

"Ha! Okay!"

"You act like you know something. What did she tell you?"

"She really didn't tell me much of shit other than what happened. When she found that condom wrapper it really hurt her, so get ready to do some beggin' cause sista girl is pissed."

"We gone see about all that. Well let me go. I hear the garage door opening now so she's home."

"Okay boo. Keep me posted."

"I'm sure if I don't, she will. Talk to you later. Thanks again for the heads up."

Hanging up with Shane, I prepared myself to deal with Ava once she walked through the door. I knew I had to get my story straight because Shane was right about one thing and that was I had slipped. I should have been way more careful than I was. While I waited for Ava to come into the house, I went to the bathroom to relieve myself. Just as I was finishing up in the bathroom, I heard the dog barking and Ava talking to him. Finishing up then washing my hands, I headed for the kitchen where she and the dog were at.

"So, look who decided to finally come home. Where have you been Ava?"

"We need to talk Justin," she replied putting the puppy down then patting and rubbing on his stomach.

I agreed a hundred percent that we needed to talk because I didn't think it was cool of her to just up and leave like she did. We ended up arguing, going back and forth cause I wasn't about to let up. She was going to tell me where she was whether she wanted to or not.

When she got to talking, "all that she needed was some time to herself" bullshit, it was starting to really piss me off. That was one of the things that frustrated me the most about Ava. She never owned up to her shit but stayed nagging the hell out of me about every little thing that I did. We were going back and forth and when she wouldn't let up and tell me where she was all those days, I chose to be the bigger person and apologize for what I had done. At the end of the day, I was wrong and should have been more careful to make sure I threw away any evidence that could get my ass caught up.

I even tried arguing the fact that she had no business searching through my shit because I never searched through her stuff, but she wouldn't let up. She just kept coming at me left and right about that damn condom wrapper that her ass shouldn't have ever seen in the first place. When I told her that she had no business rummaging through my shit, she turned into the exorcist on my ass and really went off on me. But when she got to talking about she didn't know if she wanted to still be with me, I knew I had to switch up my attitude and quickly because at the end of the day, I was wrong on all levels for what I had done. Ava was beyond pissed. So much so that me getting her a dog didn't even help me out whatsoever. Before I knew it, I was beggin' and pleading sounding like a bitch asking for her forgiveness.

What really got me was when she walked off. Talking about how she still didn't know what she wanted to do about us working things out then leaving me alone in the kitchen. At that point, I knew that I had to fight for my marriage and be on my best behavior to get her to change her mind. I loved my wife, that was no lie, but I needed her to stay with me because having her on my side made me feel manly.

I was about to follow her upstairs to see if some dick would help her change her mind, but my phone starting ringing. Picking it up off the counter and seeing that it was Tate, I decided to answer because I hadn't seen or talked to him in a few days and I wanted to catch up with him.

"What's up bro, what it do?" I answered, trying not to sound irritated behind me and Ava arguing.

"Shit nothing homie. I was just calling to see what you got going on later tonight?"

"Shit, my ass is on lockdown for a few days on the real bro. What's up with you and Dawn though? How's that going?"

"Man, she a cool chick and all, but she be acting real funny, so I left her alone. We met up and went out for a few dates, but things didn't click. She's a beautiful girl and all but I don't think she feeling me like that. What yo ass on lockdown for bro?"

"Bro don't even sweat that broad. Her ass don't be feelin' no one, not even her damn self. As long as I've known her, she ain't never had a steady man in her life. That's why I don't get why my ol' lady be telling her ass all of our business. Like, how can she help us out and give my lady any advice when the goofy ass girl can't find and keep her own man? Man bro, you know how Ava be on my ass. I fucked around and got home hella late again and she wigged out on my ass. Then being fucking careless, I left some shit in one of my pockets that she shouldn't have seen."

"Damn bro, that was harsh my dude. Tell me how you really feel about ol' girl!" Tate busted out laughing. "Yo ass a fool with it fosho. What you leave in your pockets that got your wife all bent out of shape for, bro? That's not like you to be careless."

"I'm just speaking facts bro, Dawn a whole jawn. Man, Ava fucked around and found a condom wrapper in my shit."

"Damn dude for real?"

"Straight facts bro. We been at it all week about the shit too. Then her ass pulled a disappearing act and been gone for four days. I couldn't even reach her ass cause she had her phone off the whole time and shit."

"Awww hell nah! Yo ass wild bro. Well, catch up with me when you get off punishment and shit."

"Fosho, I'll hit you back later."

"Bet."

Hanging up with Tate, I intended to go upstairs to see what Ava was up to only to be startled finding her standing in the family room off to the kitchen playing with the puppy. I hoped like hell she didn't overhear me talking about her sister to Tate, otherwise, we were going to be right back at it again, damn.

"Were you just talking to Tate?" Ava asked as she continued to play with the dog without looking up at me.

"Yeah, did you think of a name for him yet?" I asked trying to change the subject, but I could tell by her body language that she was pissed.

"I heard everything you just said about my sister. You just don't get it do you?" Ava asked.

"What don't I get Ava?"

"Why would you talk about my sister like that?"

"Come on man, let's not act like I said anything that isn't truthful about her. It's no big secret your sister hates me and she's not one of my favorites either. And, when was the last time she had a steady man in her life? I'll wait," I asked being sarcastic. "Right... never! So please don't start in on me and act like I did or said anything out of pocket about her ass."

"So, you bash my sister to your friend, and you don't think you're wrong for that?!

Wow Justin, I swear you're really something else."

"So, you don't bash me to her and your friend Shane?" I rebutted, getting fired up all over again. "Keep it real Ava. You tell your sister every damn thing about what we got going on. I believe that's why her ass don't fuck with me now."

"See, this is what I mean. I can't with you! No matter how much I try, I just can't cause you don't have no chill at all."

"You can't what?! Hell, it's not like I called him specifically to bash her ass. Tate called me and was telling me that she was acting funny towards him. Let's not sit here and act like your sister don't be with the shits with every damn body. Hell, you the only person she likes besides herself. She be talking about Shane's ass like a dog too. It's her that doesn't have any chill not me."

"Wow really J."

"Then, you say I do the most, but you eavesdropping in on my conversations, and searching my pockets and shit. What's all that shit about?"

"Obviously, it's because you do shit to make me act this way. Clear you're the one up to no good, walking around with used condoms in your pockets and coming in the house at all times of the damn night… or shall I say morning.

"You know what, you just might be right. Maybe we need some more time a part cause this shit is getting out of control."

"Ha, ya think!"

"This shit makes no damn sense to me at all! What you not gone do is sit here and act like your sister hasn't said worst about me trying to make me out like I'm the only bad person. Then, I apologized to your ass for fucking up, but you," I paused, pointing my forefinger in her face. "You never own up to your shit, ever!"

"My shit?!" Ava challenged. "I don't do shit to yo ass to cause you to act out or be concerned about what I got going on when I'm not around you. But you my nigga, you stay fucking up."

"Oh, so everything is all on me huh?"

"Yep, pretty much."

"Wow, I'm officially blown!" I huffed shaking my head in disgust. "So, you searching through my shit and telling all our business to anybody that would listen is cool. Okay, bet."

"That's not the point Justin."

"Like hell it ain't!" I bellowed causing the dog to start barking. "You over there looking all funny in the face about what you think you heard me say about Dawn's ass, but I don't hear you giving me my props for declining his invite to go hang out at his crib though. Like damn, can a brother get just an ounce of credit when it's due from your ass?"

"First off, lower your tone cause you already skating on thin ice with hot roller blades J. You're right, Dawn can't stand you no more than you can stand her, so I guess y'all are even."

"Bet. What about me choosing to stay home instead of going out to kick it? Can a nigga get his props please?"

"If you want to go out, go out. From what it sounds like to me, you're only staying in the house because we on the outs. Keep it real if nothing else! Go out if that's what you want to do. But if the sun beats your ass home, don't bother coming back."

"You can't be serious Ava."

"Oh, but I am. I'm dead ass serious as a fucking heart attack J. Try me."

"Come here," I said in my most seductive voice I could muster up. "I know what your problem is. You know you one sexy motherfucker when yo ass is mad."

Sitting behind her on the couch as she sat on the floor with the dog, I started rubbing on her back. Seeing how far she would let me go, I tried to slip my hand down the front of her shirt.

"Aht, keep your hands to yourself patna. We not cool like that."

"Damn, that's how you gone do a brother? You been gone for days! You don't miss me? Cause I missed the shit out of you."

"Stop J!" Ava giggled and I could tell she was finally starting to soften up.

Watching her play with the puppy, I could see that I made a great choice by getting the dog for her. I knew eventually that darn puppy would help soften her mood.

"Do you know what you want to name him yet?" I asked again.

"Hmmmm, what about bully?"

"Bully?! Why bully?"

"Because that's what you sounded like when you were talking about my sister to Tate. You sounded like a big ass bully!" Ava spat as she got up, picked up the dog and marched up the stairs.

"Oh my God! Have some chill will ya! Where you going now?" I asked.

"To the bedroom."

"Oh snap, let me join you. I know what you need to shake that 'tude you got."

"Don't bother! Like I said, we not cool like that. Me and my puppy the only ones going to kick in the bedroom."

"It's my bedroom too."

"It is, but you gone be camping out on the couch until further notice," she shot back.

Blowing out a deep breath, I couldn't do anything but shake my head. Tonight was about to be a long ass night for a nigga for sure.

Ava

Justin must have been out of his rabid ass mind if he thought I was going to let him touch all over me and come to the bedroom with me. Even though he had apologized and offered to go to counseling, I was still feeling uneasy about him cheating on me. Then, as if cheating wasn't enough, I caught him bashing my sister to Tate, pissing me off all over again. The only thing that he was right about when I confronted him about talking shit about my sister was the fact that they didn't like each other. I would never confirm or tell him anything that my sister had ever said about him, but she loved to bash him too.

Checking my cellphone, I saw that I had a missed call from Dawn and a text from Shane. I didn't want to call Dawn back to discuss how things went with Justin and I with him here in the house, so I decided to text her instead.

Going to the text messages, I went to see what Shane sent me first.

Shane: Hey bestie, just checking on you. I hope things are going okay

Me: Thanks bestie. We talked thing out

Shane: Great! So, did he own up to his shit?

Me: Yeah, he admitted he was wrong and apologized

Shane: So y'all working things out

Me: Sort of. I didn't kick him out and I'm not leaving as of now. I put his ass on a time out though

Shane: Well I have your back no matter what you decide

Me: thanks. I guess time will tell what happens next. I'm willing to stay and fight for our marriage if he acts right from here on out. But one more fuck up and we will be done for sure

Shane: I feel you on that hun

Me: Thanks for checking in on me

Shane: You know I got you boo

Once I was done texting Shane, I sent my sister a quick text to update her. I knew she was calling me to see how things went when I made it back home.

Me: Hey sissy, sorry I missed your call. Justin and I were talking

Dawn: So, what did he have to say for himself?

Me: He admitted he fucked up and apologized

Dawn: who is the bitch he cheated with

Me: He didn't say but at least he didn't lie about it.

Dawn: Hmmm, well I guess he apologized

Me: I know, but he promises to not let it ever happen again. He wants to work things out. He even suggested that we could go to counseling

Dawn: He is the one that needs counseling not you

Me: True dat, but at least he is trying to make things right

Dawn: I still wouldn't let his ass off the hook too soon. He shouldn't have cheated in the first place

Me: Very true

Dawn: So are you going to go to counseling with him

Me: I don't know just yet. It's not a bad idea. I'm thinking I will see how things go first though

Dawn: Let's just hope he acts right moving forward. Where is his ass at now?

Me: Downstairs. I'm in the bedroom. I'ma let him sweat it out for a few days before I completely let it go

Dawn: I don't think you should let him off so easily but I get it. Y'all are married. I just hope he doesn't do anything else stupid otherwise, I'ma have to put my foot up his ass

Me: Don't start! (laughing emoji)

Taking a picture of Bully, I sent it to Dawn

Dawn: Aww that's a cute puppy. I guess that's his, "I fucked up, will you forgive me" gift, huh?

Me: Thanks, and I guess so

Dawn: Well just keep me posted.

Me: Will do. I'll call you in the morning. Love you

Dawn: Sounds good love you too.

The one thing that I could always count on was for Dawn to keep it all the way real. It seemed like she really wasn't feeling me working things out with Justin and I could definitely understand why. What she was not understanding was I didn't get married to get a divorce, especially when we hadn't even been married a full year yet.

I planned to fight for my marriage because I had already invested so much in our relationship, but if Justin ever fucked up again and didn't get his act together, I had every intention on being done with him and for good. As far as I was concerned, I had already given him enough chances to get it right and to act like a husband. When we first got married, he showed me that he had it in him to do right. So, I guess I was going to sit back and watch. Time would tell.

It was starting to get late and I was getting hungry and tired, so I figured I'd jump in the shower then figure out what to do for dinner. Picking up my overnight bag with my dirty clothes, I went to the laundry room so that I could wash a load of clothes. Then I headed back to the bedroom to find a pair of pajamas to put on. Laying my pajamas out on the bed, I headed to the shower in hopes that a long hot shower would help me to relax.

Once I was fresh and clean, I got dressed then headed downstairs to see what I could put together for dinner. Bully must have gotten lonely while I was in the bathroom because when I got downstairs, he was hanging out with Justin. Walking into the kitchen, I was shocked to see that Justin had already ordered dinner. There were two big bags on the kitchen counter from Red Lobster.

"Hey beautiful lady, you still mad at me?"

"Really Justin, it's not about if I'm still mad at you or not. What you did was foul as fuck and I'm still unclear why you did what you did."

"Babe, can we please try to move on. How am I supposed to prove to you that I'm sorry if I have to keep back tracking to explain myself?" Justin asked with sad eyes.

"You cheated J! It's not that easy to just forgive and forget."

"I get that and again, I'm sorry. You never have to worry about me ever cheating on you again. I promise."

"Okay. I sure hope you mean that cause if you ever fuck up again, we are done. A sorry won't be able to fix shit. I hope you understand that."

"I do baby. Let's not talk about it anymore cause it won't happen again," he assured me as he walked up to me and gave me a hug. "Come on babe, you not gone hug me back?"

Giving him a hug then stepping out of his embrace, I peered at the bags of food on the counter. "I'm so glad you ordered in because I'm hungry. I came down here to see what I could put together for dinner, but you beat me to it."

"See babe, I'm showing you that I'm sorry and trying to do better already."

Justin and I started pulling out the containers of food from the bags, then we sat down to eat dinner. The whole time we sat in silence as I was thinking to myself that I surely hoped he made good on his promise to not mess up again. I truly loved my husband and it would be a shame to have to walk away from everything that we had because he couldn't act right.

Once we were done eating, we cleaned the kitchen together. Then I headed back up to the bedroom so that I could get ready for bed. We both had to work in the morning, and I was exhausted from all the arguing we had been doing.

"So, you really not going to let me sleep in the bed with you tonight."

"Nope... not a chance in hell. You can't buy me a dog and dinner and think we gone be back cool like that."

"Damn Ava, yo ass is brutal."

"I learned from the best," I retorted, looking back at him as I went up the stairs to turn in for the night.

Chapter Nine

Ava

Three Weeks Later

Things couldn't have been better over the last few weeks. Justin held true to his word and even though he still went out and kicked it with Tate on his days off, he made sure to come home at a reasonable time and that was all that I asked for. Today, I was feeling lucky because tomorrow is the first Saturday that Justin has had off in quite some time, so we had plans for a date night. I couldn't wait to finish getting my work done so that I could go home and start prepping for my special day with my man tomorrow.

Sitting at my desk wrapping up a few assignments, there was a knock on my door, distracting me from my work. I didn't have any more appointments scheduled for the day, so I wondered who it was.

"Come in!" I hollered out.

"Hey pretty lady," Kevin said as he walked into my office. "I thought I'd stop by and see how you were doing. You've been so busy we haven't had much time to catch up."

"Yeah, you're right. With the end of the semester rounding the corner I have been crazy busy to say the least. You just got back from vacation this week. How was your time off?"

"It wasn't much of a vacation. I had a death in my family."

"Oh Kevin, I'm so sorry to hear that. My condolences to you and your family. I didn't know."

"Thanks love. Yeah, my uncle that lived in New York passed away from pneumonia suddenly."

"Oh wow! I'm so very sorry to hear that," I replied as I stood up and walked from around my desk to give him a hug. "How are you holding up?"

"Oh, I'm better now. He and I were super close, so it has been hard. I'm just taking it one day at a time."

"I understand. I feel so bad. I have been so caught up in my work lately that I haven't had any extra time to stop and chit chat with you. I thought you were on vacation because you were gone for a few weeks."

"Yeah, I had to stay in New York to help my mom clean out his place and tie up a few loose ends. She and I were out in New York for a little over a week after my uncle's funeral services, then I decided to take a little time off since I had vacation time for myself to reset."

"I can truly understand that. Sounds like you and your uncle were pretty close."

"We were, he was like a second dad to me."

"Wow, I'm so sorry that he passed. I'm glad you decided to stop by to catch up."

"Yeah, I figured since you hadn't used my number and called me, I'd come check you out," Kevin said.

"Oh, about that-" I started to explain but Kevin cut me off.

"It's no biggie, you don't have to explain. How have you been though? Are things better at home?"

"Actually, they have been going pretty good. My husband and I had a long talk and thankfully, he realized what he has at home. He has been fighting to keep our marriage and was very remorseful for what he did."

"Well that's good to hear. I'm sure you taking a few days to yourself away from home helped him see that."

"It actually did, so thanks again for that."

"No thanks needed. That's what friends are for."

"Oh, and I haven't forgotten that I owe you lunch. Maybe we can go out to lunch sometime next week. Or, I can make and bring us both lunch and we can chill either in my office or the staff lounge."

"That sounds good. Welp pretty lady, I'ma head out so that I won't be stuck in all that Friday traffic."

"Ugh, I know. I'll be right behind you. I have a few more things to finish up before I leave, then I'll be heading home also. Thanks again for coming to check on me."

"Of course, and I really hope things work out for you and your husband. If you need me for anything, you got my number."

"I appreciate that."

After Kevin left, I couldn't help but to feel bad for not sending him a text to check on him. I truly thought he was on vacation and I didn't want to bother him. Hearing that he had a death in his family was just horrible. I could tell that he was still sad about it and I couldn't blame him. I was feeling a little guilty and like a bad friend for not checking in with him, but I didn't know. Plus, I was so wrapped up in my own personal life and working things out with Justin that I didn't even think to check in with him.

Once I was done with my work, I headed out of my office and straight for my car. I couldn't get home fast enough. Justin had to work today, so more than likely he wouldn't be home until later this evening. That would give me plenty of time to myself so that I could find something cute for tomorrow and fix a nice dinner tonight to kick off our weekend together. I was so happy that things were going so well between us. It really felt good to be happily married and in love.

Since I had already checked in with my sister briefly this morning, I decided to give Shane a call to see what he was up to.

"Hey bestie, how was your day?" Shane answered the phone in a very jovial tone.

"Hey hunny, my day was great. How about yours?"

"I have about six more clients to cut before I can call it a day."

"Oh, well if you're busy, just call me back later."

"Okay boo, I'll check in with you later. Love you gurl."

"Love you too," I said.

Hanging up from Shane as I sat in some light traffic, I turned the radio on. Lucky me, my favorite singer Toni Braxton's song, *I Love Me Some Him*, was on the radio. Singing along with the song, I headed home in a great mood.

Making it to the house, Bully was sitting at the door waiting on me. Dropping my bags at the door, I picked him up and started playing with him. Then I let him out the patio door so that he could go potty in the backyard while I looked for something to fix for dinner. I had forgotten to take some meat out before I left this morning, so I took out some salmon from the freezer and sat it in the sink with some cold water so that it could thaw.

Looking in the fridge, I took out two bags of spinach and kale mix then I grabbed some red skin potatoes and rinsed them off. Doing a quick peel, I cut the potatoes in half, then placed them in a pot of hot water to boil them so that I could make mashed potatoes. While the potatoes were going and the fish was thawing, I let Bully back in then headed upstairs to change out of my work clothes. Making it back down to the kitchen, the salmon was just about thawed, so I started on the mashed potatoes. Once they were done, the salmon was thawed out. Taking the filets and preparing salmon foil packets with Cajun butter, I put them in the office then sautéed the spinach and kale. Just as I was finishing up dinner, Justin walked in from work.

"Hey babe, you got it smelling good as fuck up in here."

"Thanks baby, how was work?" I asked as he kissed then slapped me on the butt.

"Work was work. How was your day?"

"It was super busy. I'm just glad it's Friday, the weekend is here, and we get to spend it together."

"I'm headed upstairs to shower and change right quick if that's cool."

"Perfect, by the time you're done, dinner will be ready."

Thirty minutes or so later, Justin was back in the kitchen smelling and looking amazing. I had just finished making our plates and fixing us some sweet tea. Sitting down at the table, we made small talk about our day as we ate.

"Whew, babe that was good."

"Thanks J, I got started on dinner as soon as I walked in. I wanted to make sure that you had a hot meal to eat when you got in from work."

"You're such an amazing wife."

"I try. Let me clean these dishes so that I can take a shower. Maybe we can find a movie to watch when I'm done."

"I'll clean the kitchen baby. You go take your shower."

"Thanks babe."

Skipping up the stairs feeling amazing, I couldn't have been happier. Making it to the bedroom, I went to my dresser to find something to put on after I showered. Deciding on a cute lil chemise that I had purchased online from Adore Me, I went into the bathroom to take a shower. Once done, I got dressed, sprayed on some Bath and Body Works peachy peach, then headed back downstairs to get my movie night on with Justin.

When I got to the family room, Justin was sitting on the couch with Bully laying at his feet while he scrolled through the TV guide.

"I don't know why I pay so much to have cable when there ain't never shit on TV," he fussed.

"Let's check Netflix. There is always something good to watch on there," I suggested.

We ended up choosing to watch, *How to Fix a Drug Scandal*. Snuggling up close to my boo, he wrapped his arm around me and I laid my head on his chest. I loved when Justin and I spent quality time together. Ten minutes into the show, we were making out, rubbing and touching all over one another.

"Let's pause the movie and go up to the bedroom for a couple of minutes," Justin purred to me.

Giggling I responded, "Last one to the room is a rotten egg."

Bolting from the couch, I darted up the stairs as fast as I could making it to the bedroom before him. We were laughing and having such a good time. All I could think was thank God we both wanted to fight for our marriage. I couldn't picture how things would have been had we gone our separate ways after he cheated.

I couldn't lie though, I frequently thought about what caused him to cheat and if he ever felt the urge to do it again. For what I could tell, he hadn't, but it was always in the back of my mind. It took me some time to get the visual of Justin having sex with another woman out of my mind, but I knew that I had to move on from it. He apologized, things were great, so there was no need to keep dwelling over it.

"You cheated!" He laughed as he lifted my chemise up taking it off.

Grabbing his t-shirt, I helped him take it off then pulled his pants down.

"I need you so bad Ava."

"Dropping to my knees, I took his hardened soul pole into my hands and started licking around the mushroom tip while sucking and stroking him.

"Ouuu fuck Ava! I love that shit."

Hearing him moan out encouraged me to get freakier, so I started deep throated his penis, going up and down while massaging his balls.

"Fuck babe, you gone make a nigga cum."

Second later, I felt a warm gush of cum fill my mouth as I swallowed, mentally patting myself on the back.

"Lay back on the bed baby. I wanna taste you," Justin demanded.

Doing as I was told, I laid back on the bed and he wasted no time diving into my core with his tongue. He sucked and slurped until my legs started vibrating and my body began to shake, The feelings coursing through my entire body I couldn't put into words if I tried. Before I knew it, I was squirting my juices all over his mouth as he continued to slurp and suck every drop of it.

I was so turned on and horny, I couldn't wait to get dicked-down by his meaty pole.

"Let me hit it from the back baby," he demanded again, but tonight I planned to take charge.

He stood up in front of me waiting to tap my ass from the back, but instead I scooted to the end of the bed and started giving him oral pleasure again. I remembered when I used to get turned off from oral sex, well giving it at least. And, I remembered when I wouldn't dare swallow, but with Justin, he had me gone. I actually enjoyed pleasing him orally because he never missed a beat showing me how much pleasure it gave him and for me, that was just the stroke to my ego that I needed to become comfortable with doing oral.

As I was doing my thing, he pulled out of my mouth and said, "Let's try something different tonight. You down?"

"Of course, I'm always down to spice it up," I responded as he reached out for my hands, helping me to stand then he got on the bed.

"I want you to suck my dick from the back," he requested.

"Come again!" I asked to be clear because I had never heard of sucking someone's dick from the back. Like how exactly would that work? Justin had a pretty big dick, but when it was erect, it pointed up not down so how was I supposed to suck his dick from the back?!

"I want you to suck my dick from the back baby. You down or what?"

"How is that going to exactly work though?"

"Look," he said as he got in the bed in the doggie style position then pushed his dick down so that I could access it easily from behind him.

Standing there looking at his ass high in the air had my stuck. I had NEVER heard of this shit before in my life, but if this was what he wanted to try I was down. My focus was on pleasing my man. Positioning myself behind him, I grabbed his dick and started sucking. It actually wasn't as bad as I thought because it gave me easier access to his balls also. Going from his dick to his balls I sucked, licked and hummed.

I could tell that Justin was enjoying every minute of it because not only could I taste his precum, but he was moaning, groaning and rocking his hips something serious. I thought it was going to be awkward since his ass was in the air, but it actually wasn't as bad as I thought, until he said...

"Lick my ass baby."

"I know you fucking lying to me!" I snapped, releasing his dick and standing up with my hands on my hips.

If he thought I was about to lick his crusty ass, he had me fucked all the way up. It was already a stretch that I was sucking his dick and balls and letting him cum in my mouth... but licking his ass! I wasn't about to do no such fucking thing.

"What's the problem babe? I thought you wanted to try something new?"

"You're fucking kidding me, right?! What do you mean lick your ass? Are you trying to be funny?"

Turning around and sitting on the bed with a look of confusion on his face he said, "Nah I'm not kidding. I'm serious babe. Just try it."

"Hell motherfucking nah I ain't!" I hissed. "I can't believe you worked up enough audacity to ask me to do some shit like that! What the fuck Justin!"

"What's the fucking problem? I lick your ass all the damn time! Why you can't return the damn favor and lick mine?"

"The fuck you mean?!"

"I'm just saying babe. You like it when I do it to you, so why can't you do ti to me? I don't see what the fuckin' problem is!!"

"Yoooo! I can't. You just turned me the fuck off. I don't know not one man that likes to get his ass licked."

"Hol' up, what you trying to say?"

"I ain't trying to say shit. I said what I said," I sneered then repeated. "I don't know one man that likes his ass licked Justin! How dare you even ask me some shit like that!"

"You said you was down to try something new."

"And I fucking did! I sucked ya dick and balls from the back. That wasn't good enough?! I had no clue you was into this type of shit."

"Yo, what you mean by that Ava? You keep throwing out this accusations and shit and we gon' have a problem."

"Shit, it means that you just blew me!"

"I personally don't see what's wrong with it. Gabrielle Union admitted on live radio that she sucks D. Wade's ass. It's a part of sex and providing the best possible pleasure to your partner Ava!"

"I don't give one rat's motherfucking monkey's ass what Gabrielle Union does! She can suck D. Wade's dick, butt, nipples... hell, she could suck whatever the fuck she wants to!! Dwyane Wade is an undercover gay man in my opinion."

"Woah, woah, woah! Don't go throwing out accusations like that when you don't know that to be factual," Justin defended.

"Well if he isn't gay, I'm positive that he is bi-sexual."

"I can't believe how closed-minded and immature you are being," Justin ranted as he marched into the bathroom.

Following behind him, I continued to let him have it.

"For the record, I am one hundred percent not being closed-minded nor am I immature. I'm not with the shit... PERIOD! And if that's the type of shit you like," I paused for a minute then continued. "Wait a damn minute! Is that why you cheated?"

"What the fuck does that have to do with anything?"

"I'm just asking. Is this the reason why you cheated?" I asked.

"I seriously think you need help. If you don't want to do it then don't. I'm sorry for even asking you to do it! Hell fuck it!"

"Yeah, fuck it! Cause ain't no way I'm ever doing no shit like that!" I spat then left out of the bathroom.

Going back into the bedroom, I grabbed my chemise from off the floor, put it back on then left out of the room. I was too done with Justin's ass. The fucking nerve of him!

Justin

I didn't know what Ava's problem was, but I was pissed off at her for making a big deal out of something so little and minor. All I was trying to do was spice things up a bit and I thought she was down for that. I licked her ass all the time. Whenever I went down on her and she loved it. Now that I was asking her to return the favor, she had a problem with it. I personally felt like she was being super selfish and the way that she reacted was totally out of line.

She was throwing out all types of slick remarks. Then when she asked me if my infidelity had something to do with me wanting my ass licked, I was instantly confused. One thing had absolutely nothing to do with the other, but it was gon' mean something today.

Finishing up in the shower, I brushed my teeth to get the smell of her pussy juices from around my mouth. Then I scurried into the bedroom so that I could get dressed. Since my wife wasn't up for doing what it took to satisfy me, then I was going to have to look out for myself as usual and go get satisfied. Sucking and fucking on her just wasn't enough to completely satisfy me. Maybe I was wrong for not telling her that directly, but I didn't want to hurt her feelings.

I knew Ava very well and had I told her that I wasn't completely satisfied with how we fucked, she would have gotten defensive about it and taken it personal. To avoid arguing about it, I just never told her in the raw like that. My way of getting that point across to her was by suggesting that we do some new shit. Clearly, she wasn't down for it.

Once I was dressed, I grabbed my cellphone so that I could text Shane to make sure that he was at home. I knew that Friday nights were one of his busiest nights at the barber shop he worked at. I wanted to make sure that he was available to hook up tonight. The reason why I wanted to reach out to Shane before checking to see if Tate was available was because certain sexual positions were off limits when it came to fucking Tate. Whereas with Shane, he was always down for whatever. I was hornier than a fuckin' goat and in need of getting pleased as opposed to having to be the pleasurer.

Me: Hey, are you home

Shane: Not yet, but I will be in about 20 minutes... why what's up

Me: I wanted to come by

Shane: Okay come on over then boo

Me: Bet. I'm on my way

Getting my wallet and keys, I headed downstairs so that I could leave. I was sexually frustrated and needed to release something serious. I was done arguing with Ava and I didn't appreciate the innuendos she was trying to imply.

"I'll be back!" I shouted, walking past the family room where Ava was sitting heading toward the garage.

"Where are you going? It's late as hell and you about to leave?"

"Out for some air. I'm not trying to argue with you no more tonight Ava."

"Argue?! I didn't realize we were arguing. I was just taken aback with you asking me to lick your ass like that. It was more of a disagreement than an argument. Is it really that serious for you to leave though?"

"Yeah, it is that serious to me!" I shouted, fully irritated that she was really sitting there downplaying the fact that she was being over dramatic. All she had to say was she was not into that and leave it at that. All that extra shit she was saying was inappropriate as hell and it had me steaming, ready to blow up on her ass.

"I really think your making this much bigger than it is and that's not cool. Instead of coming to me and talking, you wanna leave and that is bogus. We're supposed to be bigger than that."

"Well, you shoulda thought about that before you started in on my ass. But it's cool. I need some air. I'll be back," I chastised then left.

Hopping in my ride, I backed out of the garage and made my way to Shane's house.

"So, what exactly happened last night? You never did say why y'all got into it," Dawn said as I got in her car.

"I don't even want to say cause I know how you are," I replied putting on my seatbelt.

"What's that supposed to mean? What's Shane's address so I can GPS it?"

I gave her Shane's address then continued. "You know how you get whenever I tell you stuff. You hold onto that shit like it be happening to you."

"You're my little sister, so if someone fucks with you and your feelings it is happening to me chile. Just tell me what happened."

"Justin and I were being intimate, and he asked me to not only suck his dick from the back, but he wanted me to lick his ass too. I snapped out and he-"

"Woah, woah, woah! Yoooo, sis! He asked you to do what?" Dawn interrupted looking over at me like I had offended her.

"You heard me right. He asked me to lick his ass," I repeated. "Trust me, I had the same reaction and the same look on my face that you have right now."

"But hol' up! I ain't never heard of sucking dick from the back. How the fuck that shit even work?"

"I've never heard about it until last night either."

"I'm sitting here really trying to figure this shit out cause when a dick gets hard that joker sticks either straight out, up, or to the side. What kind of dick that nigga got-"

"Dawn please! You starting to do too much."

"Nah, that shit is too much! So, did you do it?"

"I gave him oral from behind, but I wasn't about to lick his damn ass!"

"How in the hell did you manage to do it though. I'm really not trying to be all up in y'all's business or no shit, but this is some shit I need to know. Is that really possible?"

"Yes, it's possible. He got on the bed in the doggie style position and I grabbed his dick from behind him and pulled-"

"Girl, stop! I done heard enough! Ain't no fucking way I'm putting my face close to no nigga's ass like that. You a real one forreal, forreal! So that nigga likes his ass to be licked too?! Chile! This is too damn much for me! I would have round house his him right in his ass!"

"I swear you do the most. You just say whatever comes to your mind, not giving one damn!"

"So, you gone act like that's not too much! Let me find out that fool like it in the booty! Let me find that shit out and it's gonna be a fucking problem tah-day!"

"See now you got me thinking cause I don't know very many men that like to have their ass licked,"

"Or dick sucked from the back bitch! Don't leave that part out like that shit is okay."

"Will you chill?! The sucking dick from the back part isn't as bad as you think."

"That's your story boo."

"I'm just saying, yeah it's different but it doesn't mean that he likes it in the booty sis. It's really not all that you making it seem. Now the licking his ass part, that got me feeling some type of way. I was completely taken off guard and offended to say the least."

"I bet you were!" Dawn interjected. "Boy, that fool lucky he pulled that shit with you. I wish a motherfucker WOULD ask me some shit like that."

"Don't start-"

"Don't start what?" Dawn asked, cutting me off. "That clown tried you!"

"He definitely did that because he snapped and left and hasn't been back home since."

"I thought that he didn't care for or liked Shane?"

"He doesn't," I responded.

"So, what in the hell would he be doing at his house if he doesn't like that nigga?"

"Now, that's the smartest question you asked me all day cause I'm sitting here wondering the same thing. I called Shane before I called you and he never answered my call, nor has he called me back."

"This shit getting juicier and juicier by the second. Let me find out they over there fucking on each other. I'ma beat both of their asses. Straight like that!"

"Justin is not gay Dawn. Just because he is here now, doesn't mean that he has been here since last night. And it certainly doesn't mean they over there fucking on each other either!" My sister had a really wild imagination if she thought my husband was in there fucking my best friend. That would be some insane shit, but I was really trying to figure out why Justin was here though.

"Facts! But how long does the app say he has been here?"

"I didn't know that it would tell you all of that. I swear you're like a technology wizard."

"Shit, nowadays you have to be for times like this!" Dawn laughed.

Pulling up the Life 360 app on my phone, I checked to see if it would tell me when Justin arrived at Shane's house. When it said that he had been here since last night, I gasped out loud.

"What it say, bitch shit!?"

"I don't even want to say," I responded.

Before I could say anything else, Dawn had done snatched my cellphone out of my hand and looked for herself.

"Oh, now see, I'ma hafta kill both they asses!" I shouted. "See, I told you Shane's ass couldn't be trusted. I knew there was a reason why I didn't like his ass. You need to be more careful when you select your friends, and men cause this shit is too damn much. I'm sorry sis, but I ain't gone chill on none of that! Both of them finna get these hands as SOON as I pull up to the house... on God!"

I couldn't do anything but sit there and take all that she was saying in because she was right. She never really cared for Shane nor Justin and if there wasn't a good enough reason for Justin to be at Shane's house, then they both had proven her right all along. As I sat there deep in my thoughts, trying not to become emotional while Dawn drove like a bat out of hell to Shane's, all I could do was pray to God that nothing inappropriate was going on.

When we pulled up to Shane's house, Dawn barely parked her car correctly as she slammed on her breaks and jetted out the car.

"Wait! Dawn, wait a damn minute!" I yelled out to her, not ready to be faced with what was really going on.

"Wait for what?" she asked, looking at me like I was crazy.

"Let's just sit in the car and wait for Justin to leave."

"Girl you sound crazy as hell. But hold up," she said, coming back to the driver's side, opening the door and popping her trunk.

Getting out of the car, I went to go see what she was doing.

"What are you looking for?" I asked as she searched through her trunk.

"Something to beat they ass with. They not about to get off easy this time."

"Let's just see what's going on first before you go jumping to conclusions."

"I ain't tryna hear it. Either way, we about to be prepared for some shit to pop off," Dawn replied. "Fuck! I can't find my damn bat! Shit, this double dutch rope gone have to work."

"What are you doing with a double dutch rope in your trunk?"

"Girl it's good exercise. Me and a few of my friends meet up and jump every once in a while. You should come with us one day," Dawn replied separating the two ropes handing me one then walking off toward Shane's front door. "Come on, why you just standing there? Now ain't the time for you to be getting all soft. You damn husband in there fucking your gay ass bestie!"

Speed walking to catch up to Dawn, all I could think was *Lord, please don't let this be what I think it is.* As soon as Dawn got to the front door, she started ringing Shane's doorbell and knocking on the door at the same time.

It took a good ten minutes before we heard what sounded like Shane's voice coming to the door.

"Who the hell ringing my shit and knocking on my damn door like the fucking police!" We heard Shane say right before he swung the door open. "What in the hell!"

"Where he at?" Dawn shouted. "The fuck is Justin's ass at?"

"What the hell is going on?" Shane asked looking from me to Dawn.

"That's what we're trying to find out," I answered. "Where is Justin at Shane and why is he at your house?"

"Whaa... Whaaat you mean-" Shane tried to ask, but by then Dawn had pushed him out the way and walked into his house.

"Justin! Justin! Bring your ass out here motherfucker!" Dawn yelled.

"Why would you think he is here though?" Shane asked.

"Stop playing Shane. His car is parked two houses down. Where else would he be?" I asked giving him a mean mug. "The real question is what is going on between you two?! Why has my husband been over here since last night?"

"I, I, I, I don't know what you talking about," Shane stuttered.

Before any of us could say anything else, Justin came walking up to the front door putting his shirt on with his pants unzipped.

"You dirty motherfucker you!" I spat, barging into the house further confronting Justin. "What the fuck! What are you doing here Justin?" I asked and before he could answer, my reflexes had got the best of me and I swung the rope that was in my hand at him, hitting him across his face and chest. "You fucking Shane now?!" I asked as I continued swinging the rope.

"What the fuck!" Was all Justin could say as he continued to try to cover himself as I whooped his ass with the rope.

As I was whooping Justin's ass, Dawn was giving Shane the ass whipping of his life. The whole time she was fussing and cussing him out calling him all types of names. Somehow, Justin was able to grab ahold of the rope preventing me from hitting him.

"Let me explain, it's not what you think," he pleaded.

"What's to explain? You come walking up in here, putting your clothes on and shit. I can't believe you!" I cried.

As Justin stood there trying to come up with a good enough excuse, Shane had somehow broke free from the ass whooping Dawn was giving him.

"I'm calling the police!" Shane bellowed.

Shane was fair skinned, so you could tell that Dawn had really got his ass good because his face, chest and arms were bright red with welts all over him. I knew that Justin was lying when he said that nothing was going on because Shane only had on a pair of boy shorts.

"I'm so sorry Ava! I never meant for you to find out like this," Shane admitted then continued. "But I'ma have to ask you to get your guard dog under control or I'ma have to call the police on y'all.

"Guard dog!" Dawn shouted as she swung the rope and hit him across his back. "You over here doing God knows what with my sister's husband! You lucky I don't kill yo nasty ass. And you!" she shouted pointing her finger at Justin. "You ought to be ashamed of yourself! You have a wife and you over here fuckin' this nigga!!"

"Come on Dawn. Let's go. I've seen all I need to see. As for you," I said pointing to Justin. "We are done! There's no coming back from this shit." To show him that I meant business, I took off my wedding ring and threw it in his face.

"Ava!" Justin called out at the same time as Shane. "Ava baby please!"

"I don't have shit to say to either one of y'all. Fuck both you punk ass niggas!" I spat as Dawn and I left, slamming Shane's door behind us.

As we walked back to Dawn's car, a few of Shane's neighbors were standing out on their front porches being nosey, but I didn't care. My feelings were hurt. Justin had fucked up for the last time. As for Shane, I couldn't even think clearly to know what to do about his ass. All I knew for sure was that our friendship was over as well.

Chapter Eleven

Justin

When I left home last night, I was more than 380 degrees hot with Ava's ass. To say that I was frustrated and I needed to release some stress would be an understatement. I ended up spending the night at Shane's and just as I needed, he delivered all the pleasure and then some that Ava was too much of a prude to give. We fucked and he sucked my dick from the back so good making sure to lick every inch of my ass at the same time, that I was in complete bliss.

The both of us were so caught up in pleasing one another that time got away and before I knew it, we had fucked damn near all night long. By the time we were done, we both passed out from exhaustion. We didn't wake up until we heard someone knocking on Shane's front door while ringing his bell.

"I wonder who in the fuck knocking on my door like they done lost their damn mind," Shane spat, getting out of bed then going to see who it was.

As I laid in bed, never in a million and one years did I ever expect for it to be my wife and her sister. I had absolutely no clue how she figured out that I was at Shane's house, but she had, and she was pissed. When I heard both Ava and Dawn's voices, I leaped out of Shane's bed and rushed to put on my clothes as I headed to the front of the house.

One thing led to another and before I knew it, Dawn was beating Shane's ass and Ava was swinging on me with some kind of rope. She ended up getting in a few good licks too. I had welts across my arms, face and somehow, she had busted my lip. I tried to calm her down so that I could talk to her, but with Dawn there as her hype man, I was screwed. When Shane threatened to call the police, Dawn finally got off him and then she and Ava left. I wanted to run out the house after her, but when I got to the door, some of Shane's neighbor's were out front and I was already embarrassed enough.

"What the fuck just happened?! I told you that you needed to be more careful! Now look what you done did!" Shane bellowed, tending to the cuts on his arm at the kitchen sink. "My best friend probably hates my guts and it's all your fault!"

"My fault! Motherfucka it's both of our faults! You just as wrong as I am. You over here worried about losing a friend and shit when I'm the one losing my wife."

"As if you really give a fuck about that. You said yourself that Ava doesn't completely satisfy you. Stop lying to yourself and everyone else around you. If you really loved her and didn't want to lose her, you wouldn't be over here in my bed fucking on me! You're just mad that the cat has been let out the bag about you being bi-sexual."

"You don't know what you're talking about. I have way more at risk than you!" I argued.

"How you figure that shit?! I just possibly lost the best friend that I ever had-"

"If you were so concerned about losing your best friend why in the fuck were you fucking and sucking on me!?" I countered. "I'm out! I gotta go try to calm Ava down."

"You sure that's a good idea?"

"Why wouldn't it be?" I asked.

"She had her guard dog in tow. You must want that ass beat again. If you think Dawn ain't gone be waiting on your ass when you get home, you dumber than I thought. Your best bet is to wait it out for a while."

"Unlike you, I ain't scared of Dawn's ass."

"I ain't scared of her either! I had no clue she was going to Mayweather my ass like that. Had I known and been prepared, she would have gotten her ass kicked."

"Yeah right! From where I was standing, you were howling and crying like a little bitch."

"Nigga, fuck you!" Shane fussed.

"I'm just saying. How the fuck did she even know that I was over here?"

"How the hell do I know?"

"I'm just saying. How was she able to figure that out unless you been in the streets talking?"

"In the streets talking to who though dummy?! Ava is my best friend! Why on earth would I tell anyone that I'm fucking her husband stupid!"

"Nigga watch your mouth with all that name calling."

"Nigga fuck you! You can get your shit and get tah stepping! Yo ass was howling and crying out also! I told yo ass to be more careful! But nah, you thought this shit was a joke. Take yo ass on home so you can get another beat down. I'm over this shit. I mean really! Look at my face!" Shane all but cried as he looked at his face in the full-length body mirror in the hallway leading from the kitchen to his bedroom. "Look at all these fuckin' welts on my body! Ugh! This is all your fuckin' fault!"

Going into his bedroom, I grabbed my things and got ready to leave. I wasn't about to go back and forth with Shane about who was right and wrong or who had more to lose. I had bigger issues to be concerned with and that was trying to convince Ava that it wasn't what she thought. The last thing that I needed was for her and her sister to go parading around town telling people they caught me and Shane together.

"I'll holla!" I spat as I walked out of Shane's front door before he could answer then headed to my car.

Getting in my car, I sat there trying to figure out how Ava knew where I was at. If Shane wasn't out running his mouth, how did she figure it out? Grabbing my cellphone, I tried calling Ava. I figured I could get her to talk to me instead of fighting and having to be confronted by her sister if she was at my house. The call went straight to voicemail letting me know that she had me on block.

"Damn, damn, damn!" I shouted as I hit my steering wheel.

Taking a chance, I headed to my house in hopes that Ava was there alone so that she and I could talk. I didn't need to have Dawn all up in my business, so I hoped that she was not there. But as luck would have it, Dawn's car was parked in our driveway. Shaking my head, I pulled off then called Tate, praying he would be home.

"What's up bro?" Tate asked, answering the phone.

"Hey dude, are you at home?"

"Yeah, you coming by?"

"Oh, thank God!" I rejoiced. "Yeah man, I'm on my way."

"Is everything okay?"

"Man, hell nah!"

"What done happened now?" Tate asked.

"Dude, you wouldn't believe me if I told you."

"Try me." He laughed, not realizing that I was dead ass serious.

"Man, Ava caught me at her friend Shane's house."

"The gay dude she be hanging with?"

"Yea bro!"

"J, what the hell man! I didn't know you were fucking around with dude. When did that shit start?"

"A while ago bro."

"Damn dude, why would you play with fire like that?" Tate asked.

"Man, it just happened. I feel fucked up about the shit too cause I never thought she would find out."

"How did she find out?"

"She and I got into an argument last night and I left and went to Shane's. I ended up spending the night. The next thing I know, she showed up at his front door with Dawn this morning."

"WORD!" Tate exclaimed. "How the hell did she know you were over there?"

"I wish I knew," I pondered.

"That shit sounds like a set up. Do you think dude set you up?"

"Nah, cause the way her sister was beating his ass, I believe they were just as surprised to see me at his house as we were to see them."

"Damn bro, that's some crazy ass shit."

"Tell me about it. Now Ava talking about we done with and for some reason, I believe her this time. The look of her face, I saw in her eyes were totally different than I had ever seen before. Not just that, but she took off her rings and threw them at me before she left. Man, I really fucked up this time!"

"Damn, I don't even know what to say. I'm still lowkey tripping off the fact that you and ol' boy was fucking around. Never would I have ever guessed that shit. I always thought y'all couldn't stand one another."

"Nah man, we couldn't let Ava know we were cool like that. Of all the dumb shit I could think to do, why on earth did I have to let this shit happen?!"

"That's a very good question. So, what are you going to do now?"

"I have no idea. For one, I'm not about to go to the house right now with Dawn over there. She already knows enough as it is. I'd rather talk to Ava alone than to address this all in front of her sister."

"I feel you on that. Well, you're welcome to come over here for as long as you need."

"Thanks T, I appreciate that. Thank God you're not at work."

"I actually just got off this morning. I'm off until Monday."

"Shit, tonight Ava and I were supposed to be having a date night. I can take an educated guess that that shit ain't about to happen."

"Nope, probably not."

"Fuck! I can't believe this shit! I'm about to pull up to your crib now. See you when I get there."

Hanging up with Tate, I parked my car in front of his house then went to his door. I was so grateful that he was at home because otherwise, I would have had to put money on a hotel room. There was no way in hell I was going back to the house with Dawn's ass there. Hopefully, she would leaving soon though because I needed to work in the morning, and I wanted to talk this over with Ava instead of worrying about it and leaving it the way that it was now.

Ava

One Week Later

"Good morning sis, how are you feeling?" Dawn asked, yawning at the same time.

"Hey, I'm feeling okay. How are you?" I asked, standing in the bedroom doorway of Dawn's bedroom.

Me and Bully had been staying at her house ever since I caught Justin at Shane's house.

"My first two appointments canceled on me, so I'ma lay like broccoli for another hour or two."

"Lucky you. I'm anxious to get my day started. I only work a half day today because I have an appointment to see that divorce lawyer," I said, walking up to her dresser then checked my hair in the mirror.

Checking out the different perfumes she had laid out on her dresser, I picked up a bottle of Gucci Bamboo and sprayed a little on my neck and wrists.

"I'm so glad you're still going through with the divorce. I still can't believe those two idiots. You need to start taking heed a little more to what I be saying. When I get a bad feeling about someone, I'm usually on point. My intuition don't be playing no games."

"Shit you can't believe them! How do you think I feel? I hear you and I do listen. I just think it's your delivery. You be so adamant about shit and the way you be saying stuff sometimes, you be doing the most."

"Yeah, but you know me and you know how I am. I like to give it straight up no chaser. I don't be having time for the bullshit at all. Your hair is super cute today. I did a damn good job on that silk wrap this time."

"Yeah you did. You are the best at what you do for sure."

"Thanks boo. Now, if you start listening to my advice more, your life will be much more peaceful. I promise."

"Oh lawd, let me head to work before you get started. Are you taking Bully to the shop with you today or leaving him here?" I asked.

"Shit I'ma take his little ass with me. I ain't leaving that dog here alone so he can tear up my house!" Dawn expressed.

"Oh, stop it! He's not that bad, he's just a puppy."

"He's just a puppy my ass! That damn dog worse than a pack of two-year-old kids. His ass gets into every damn thing with his spoiled self!"

"I'll call you and keep you updated on what the lawyer says."

"Ok cool. Love you!"

"Love you too!" I responded then gathered my things so I could head to work.

On the drive in, I couldn't help but to think about everything that had taken place and reminisce on the fact that my marriage was over for good. I never thought that I would be meeting with a divorce attorney in under a year of getting married. I couldn't help but to feel like a failure in some ways. I was still in shock that I had caught Justin at Shane's house. I couldn't believe the betrayal of both of them. Never in my wildest dreams would I have ever guessed that Justin of all people would not only sleep with a man, but my so called best friend at that. I once heard the saying, "Don't tell your friends anything about your man's bedroom skills". I just never thought I'd have to worry about that with Shane.

When Dawn and I left Shane's house that day, we went back to my house and waited for Justin to get home. Once nightfall came, I figured he wasn't going to show up, so Dawn offered for me and Bully to come stay with her until I figured out what I was going to do. I knew that no matter what Justin had to say for himself, I wasn't going to stay with him in that house for a minute longer. For him to cheat on me that first time was more than enough, but to find out that it was with Shane was just too damn much to deal with. Some things just weren't forgivable and for me, that was one of those things.

I ended up blocking Justin from calling me because I was so angry and disgusted with his ass. I knew that he was going to try to call me to plead his case, but nothing he could say mattered anymore at this point. The truth was finally in the open and the way I saw it, there was no coming back from it. There could never be no me and him ever again. If he preferred to sleep with men, that was his prerogative. I wasn't going to judge that, but at the same time I didn't want no parts of it. Then for him to mess with Shane, who kept a flock of different men that he fucked around with, was just nasty to me.

Justin had me questioning everything about our relationship. How could he have had me thinking that he loved me when he preferred to be with a man? It had become too much to deal with and I knew that our relationship was over with for good. At this point, there wasn't anything in my opinion that he could say that could fix the damage that was done.

Then there was Shane's disloyal ass. The audacity of him to prance around in face, phony kicking it when the whole time he was sleeping with my husband. He was way out of order for that shit. He had been calling me every day since I caught his ass and even though I wanted to hear him out, I just couldn't bring myself to talk to him yet. I was too angry, upset and hurt.

I felt betrayed in the worst way because I had confided in Shane more than I did my own sister about me and Justin and the woes of my relationship. Now, he had me thinking that he was relishing in my pain because how else could he be there to console me then turn around and sleep with my man like that. All the times that I called and vented to him about what was going on in my relationship just for him to turn around and fuck my husband was nothing but a pure disgrace.

I was thankful that my sister let me come and stay with her because the only other option I had was to go to the hotel that I had stayed at when I first left Justin and it wasn't cheap. Then another problem with that was they didn't allow for any dogs to stay at the hotel and I wasn't about to leave my Bully with Justin's sick ass.

My sister helped me pack as much of my belongings as I could the night that I left. I had been staying in her spare room at her house while looking for either an apartment or house to rent. I even called Kevin and told him about what happened. To my surprise, he said since the whole condom debacle, he knew eventually something else would happen. He figured it would only be a matter of time before my husband fucked up again. Kevin was convinced that Justin didn't value or appreciate me as his woman.

When I told him how I had caught Justin with Shane, he was speechless. Ever since then, not only did we see each other at work every day, but we had been talking to each other almost daily on the phone. Kevin had become a very good friend of mine who stayed encouraging and uplifting me every opportunity he got. Even though he still lightweight flirted with me, he respected the fact that I was still married and never crossed any lines with me. In a way, I appreciated the fact that he would flirt with me because it sort of made me feel good in a way.

Finding out that my husband was cheating on me was one thing. Finding out he was cheaing on me with a man really did a number to my self-worth and self-esteem. I started questioning everything about myself; was I not good enough, pretty enough, sexy enough? But Kevin always provided me with the assurance that I was more than enough and for that I truly appreciated him.

Today, I was scheduled to meet up with a lawyer to finally draw up my divorce papers. I didn't want anything from Justin but my maiden name and my dog. Even though my sister said I should fight him for my cut of his benefits and retirement from his job, I didn't think it was worth it. I didn't want to have any more ties to him once the divorce was final. He could keep his house. I just wanted the rest of my belongings and some of the furniture that was in it because some of it was mine that I had moved in we got the house.

We had a joint banking account that we paid the bills from, where part of his payroll check and mine was deposited into, the majority of my money went into my own personal account. The day after I left our house, I went to the bank and transferred half of what was in our joint account into my personal account then put in the paperwork to take my name off of the joint account. Like I said, I wanted no ties to Justin. I just wanted to be done entirely and completely with his ass.

Pulling into a park, I grabbed my things and headed inside. The sooner I could get my day going, the faster it would be over, and I could get to the lawyer's office.

"Good morning beautiful. You look happy and well rested."

"Good morning Kevin. I am very well rested. I was able to get some good sleep last night."

"That's good to hear. So today is the big day, huh?"

"Yep and I can't wait to get those divorce papers drawn up and for all of this to be over with."

"I feel you on that baby girl."

"I brought us some Cajun pasta that I made last night for lunch."

"Oh yeah! I'm looking forward to checking out your cooking skills since you say you can burn in the kitchen." Kevin smiled.

"Well, let me get to work. I have a few things to finish up."

"Ok sweetie, I'll see you at lunchtime."

Heading inside, I went straight to my office. I had a few reports to write up that I needed to have done today before I left. Lucky for me, the day went fast, just like I prayed for it to do. Lunchtime had approached and all I had left to do was have lunch with Kevin then I would be on my way to see the lawyer. Woohoo!

Turning my computer off, I headed to the teachers' lounge so that I could heat up the pasta that I cooked last night. When I was done, I headed back to my office to wait for Kevin. I didn't want to sit in the teachers' lounge to eat because I didn't want anyone to be all up in our business. Sometimes our conversations had a lot of tea and what we discussed needed to stay between he and I.

As I sat and waited for Kevin to get to my office, my cellphone started ringing. Checking to see who it was, I saw that it was Shane. I really didn't want to be bothered with him, and even though I wanted to hear him out, I just wasn't ready to talk to him yet. But, since he was being relentless and calling me multiple times in a day and seeing that he had called me already four times today alone, I went ahead and answered to see what he had to say for himself.

"Oh my God! Hunny, thank you so much for answering my call. I have been calling and calling-"

"You can chill on all of that hunny shit, Shane. I think it's pretty obvious why I haven't been answering your calls. Because of you my marriage is over, so to be quite frank and honest, I really don't have shit to say to your ass. You keep blowing my damn phone up that's the only reason why I even answered."

"I get that Ava, and I'm so very sorry for what I did. I promise you that I will explain it all to you."

"Okay, start explaining," I replied as I rolled my eyes. I wanted to scream and cuss his ass out, but I had to be mindful of the fact that I was still at work.

"I promise I will. I just think that's a conversation that we should have face to face."

"Aht, I'm not ready to be face to face with you just yet. I wanna kick ya ass to be truthful."

"Aye mama, I know, and you have every right to feel that way. I want to kick my own ass for betraying you like that. I was hoping that you would be available today when you get off of work. I really need you right now," Shane cried. "I wanted to know if you could come over and pick me up. I have been here sick to my stomach. I don't know what is going on with me, but I feel awful and I really need you right now. I went to the doctor last week and had to get some tests ran. I truly believe I might have some kind of cancer or something. My doctor called me back today. My results are in and they won't give them to me over the phone which has me stressing like hell. I have to go into the office for my results and I really don't want to go alone."

"Are you fucking serious right now? I'm sorry you're going through whatever it is you're going through, but you have a lot of fucking nerve Shane. You betrayed our friendship by fucking my husband and now you have the gall to ask me for a fucking favor?! Go to hell Shane, real talk!"

"Please Ava, I need you! I really think something is seriously wrong with me. I know that I fucked up and you probably hate my guts right now, but I truly feel that this is a matter of life and death. I don't have anyone else to call! You're my only friend!"

"We aren't friends anymore. Let's be clear on that!" I scoffed.

"I don't have anyone else-"

"Why don't you call Justin?" I interrupted. "You guys seemed pretty close last time I saw y'all!"

"Okay, I deserve that. Please, could you please find it in your heart to come with me."

"I don't know Shane. I'm really not feeling you or what you have going on right now."

"I know and I totally understand. But please, I know your heart and you have a heart of gold. Please, please, please just come with me this one time and I promise you won't ever have to talk to me again after this," Shane continued to plead.

"I'm still sitting here trying to figure out why the fuck you calling me with this shit. We're not friends anymore. What's going on with you is no longer a concern of mine."

"Ava please," Shane cried. "I really think it might be cancer. I have been sick and in excruciating pain. Something is terribly wrong with my body... I just know it," Shane boohooed. "You know how cancer runs in my family on both sides. I'm terrified Ava, please! I can barely walk! I'm in so much pain!"

In all the years that Shane and I had been friends, not once had I ever heard him cry about anything like he was doing today. He was right, cancer did run on both sides of his family. Over the years, he had lost quite a few of his family members from cancer, so I could see why he was so concerned. As much as I wanted to tell his ass to go play in traffic during rush hour, I couldn't. Plus, if nothing else, I wanted to hear him out. I needed to know why he betrayed our friendship like he did when I had done nothing but be the best friend I could with him.

"Ugh! What time is your appointment? Because I have an important appointment scheduled for today that I cannot and will not miss for anything or anyone."

"My doctor's office is open late today, but the earliest they could get me in is at 5:30."

"My appointment is at 3:00. If I'm done by then, I will come pick you up."

"Ahhhhh!" Shane screamed out. "Thank you so much. Thank you, thank you."

"Don't go getting yourself too excited cause if my appointment runs late, you gone be shit out of luck."

"Okay, okay. I would really appreciate it if you can come. If you can't, I understand. I'll just have to take an Uber or Lyft."

"Yeah whatever."

Just as I was hanging up with Shane, not giving him a chance to keep begging me, Kevin walked into my office.

Chapter Twelve

Shane

When Ava and Dawn showed up to my house and caught Justin over here, I could have died right there on the spot. Not only was I embarrassed but I felt terrible. I knew that I shouldn't have been fucking around with Justin, but I wasn't thinking with the right head when we first started. To be honest, I was so caught up in the physical moment and taken aback that Justin was even interested in me that it just happened. Once we went there, it was like he became an addiction to me just as much as I was to him.

Just like Ava would come to me and vent about the things that would go on in their relationship, Justin had started doing the same thing. One of things that I was most surprised by was the fact that when he and Ava would have sex, he wouldn't be completely satisfied. His whole undercover, down low sex life really was a shock to me because I always looked at him as a full heterosexual man. Even when Ava would boast about their sexual escapades, she never once told me that he complained about not being satisfied. This had all became too much for me and before I knew it, I was so caught up in such a tangled web that I had no clue how to get out of it. Actually, I wasn't even looking to get out of it any time soon, and that was the sad part about it all.

Justin tried to put all of the blame on me when we got caught, but the truth of the matter was we were both wrong. We had no business sneaking around like we were, but when I thought about it, I really felt that I was a much better match for Justin than Ava was anyway. I also believed that Justin felt the same way, but he was too busy trying to be on the DL to see that. It was just an overall messed up situation for us all and I truly regretted my actions.

Ever since the day we got caught, Justin and I hadn't been seeing each other. Plus, I had started to not feel good. At first, I thought I was just overly stressed out and coming down with a cold. Then I thought that maybe my allergies were getting the best of me. But then my body started to ache. I was feeling tired as hell all of the time too, and it seemed like every time I would eat, I was racing to the bathroom to take a shit. As I started to feel worse, it began to interfere with me being able to be as productive as I would usually be at work. I was always feeling nausea and different smells would make me feel sick to the stomach.

I remember when my mom and uncle had cancer and how they would have similar symptoms that I was feeling. My mom died from brain cancer and my uncle died from stomach cancer. His stomach cancer symptoms really had me feeling spooked, which was why I buckled down and made an appointment with my doctor. I was petrified thinking why me Lord, but at the same time thinking this was my karma coming to bite me in the ass for fucking around with not just Ava's husband, but all of those other men. It seemed like every man I was with was either already in a relationship, on the DL or married on the DL. When they said that karma was a bitch, they ain't never lied.

I knew Ava was feeling like I was being very selfish by calling her and asking her to come along with me to the doctor and I guess in a way and considering the circumstances, I was. But I didn't have anyone else in my life that was close to me like she was that I trusted to come with me. I felt that if my test results showed that I had cancer, I was going to lose my shit and because of that, I didn't want to go alone. Also, I was in so much pain and the pain medication and antibiotics that my doctor prescribed to me weren't working. He couldn't really give me anything more than what he gave me because I didn't have a full diagnosis just yet.

For Ava to agree to go with me if she finished with her appointment on time was a true blessing and testament to the fact that she had a heart of gold. Which in turn really had me feeling very fucked up for sleeping around with Justin, but I couldn't change or undo what was already done.

As I waited with baited bells on for Ava to pick me up, I prayed that once we talked, we would be able to salvage some of the friendship that we once had. I just hoped she didn't bring her sister along for the ride cause me and that wench were on the outs. She didn't know it yet, but as soon as I figured out what was going on with me and got to feeling better, Dawn had an ass whoopin' coming to her, on life.

In my opinion, she had no business getting all up in the mix that day. I got that she was Ava's sister and all, but still Justin wasn't her man, so it wasn't her battle to fight. But it was cool though because like I said, Dawn done wrote a check that her ass wasn't going to be able to cash cause I planned on beating that ass on sight.

Checking the time, I saw that it was a quarter to five. Just as I was about to call for an Uber, Ava called me.

"I'm outside."

"Thank you so much! I'm on my way out now. Are you alone?" I asked, checking to see if she brought her guard dog along for the ride.

"Ah yeah, who else would I be with?" Ave snapped back.

"I just wanted to make sure hunny. I'm really not well enough to be having to fight anybody off of me today."

"If you're asking about Dawn, she is not with me. But she should be the least of your worries. You betta come on out before I change my mind."

"Okay, I'm coming now."

Hanging up with Ava, I suddenly became super nervous. She and I have had disagreements in the past, but we had never fallen out like this before. I had seen and heard her upset many of times with Justin, but it was never directed toward me, so I really didn't know what to expect. Plus, the fruit didn't fall too far from the tree and knowing how reckless and crazy her sister was, I figured Ava had that same potential. I was in no condition to be physically fighting with anyone.

Making it out to her car, I took a deep breath then got in.

"Hey, I really appreciate you doing this for me."

"You should because I started not to come," Ava stated as she quickly glanced over to me. "You really look like shit. I hope your ass ain't got the flu cause the last thing I need is to be getting sick."

"It's not the flu. Plus, I have been on a round of antibiotics for the past week. If I was contagious, I'm not anymore."

"I hope not. Where is your doctor's office located?"

After rattling off my doctor's address, we just sat in silence. The tension was so thick it could be cut with a knife. Thinking I needed to be the bigger person in this case, I figured I should at least explain myself.

"Look, I know that things are off with us right now-"

"Ya think?!" Ava interrupted.

"You have every right to hate me right now. Hell, I hate myself for what I did. I shouldn't have ever gone there with Justin like that. I am truly sorry for betraying you, I don't even know how to put into words how sorry I am."

"My whole thing is, how did it all start? Like, who made the move on who? Then for you to pretend to be my friend not once telling me what was going on has me feeling really fucked up right now. It's totally got you looking like a snake in my eyes. I could never ever trust you after this. I hope you know and understand that."

"I totally get it. I will tell you everything. Whatever you want to know just ask."

"You can start by answering the questions I just asked you."

"Well, one night, Justin came to the shop for a haircut and he got to rambling about you and him getting into it. When he got to talking about y'all's sex life, I was shocked as hell because I honestly always thought that he didn't like me. He was my last appointment that day and I was closing the shop, so we were alone and the next thing I knew he made a move on me."

"Wow! You expect me to believe that Justin made the first move when I know how much of a ho you are!"

"Ouch! That was harsh."

"Harsh how?! Let's not act like you're not a ho. You're the one always telling me about this and that guy that you be hooking up with. Unless you been lying. My thing is, if my husband made a move on you, why would you one, not stop him and two, not tell me?"

"Like I said Ava, and I'm being brutally honest with you. One thing led to another and it just happened. I wasn't thinking straight at all. I had a little brown liquor in me too. You know how we be drinking and shit at the shop. I wasn't thinking clearly and before I knew it, we both crossed the line. It was too late for me to take back."

"So, you just kept hooking up with him knowing that he and I were together though?!"

"I mean yes. According to him, he wasn't sexually satisfied with you. I hate to say that out loud because I feel that it's his place to tell you that, but your husband is on the DL Ava."

"All those times I would call you crying a river about him being out and suspecting that he was cheating on me, you knew! You knew enough information to free my concerns about what he had going on and not one time did you ever say anything."

"I'm so sorry."

"SORRY IS NOT GOOD ENOUGH!" Ava shouted causing me to jump in my seat. "This shit y'all pulled is unforgivable."

"I know it's going to take you some time to get past all of this."

"Some time?! Nigga I ain't ever gonna get past that shit. Two people that I thought I loved and loved me back betrayed me in the worse way. Don't you get that?!"

"I totally get it. You have every reason to feel the way that you feel. If I could turn back the hands of time, I would. I hate myself for making you feel that way."

"Hmph."

As we pulled into a parking spot at my doctor's office, I got ready to get out of the car, but Ava was sitting there like she wasn't going to come in.

"You're coming in, right?"

"I hadn't planned to. You need me to come in too?"

"Yeah, that's why I wanted you to come. I just have a bad feeling about this. I feel like I'm going to be told I have cancer and I really want you there."

"Ugh!" Ava blew out a long frustrated breath then got out of the car.

After checking in and paying my copay, Ava and I sat and waited for me to be called to the back.

"Shane Brown!" a nurse called out.

"Here goes nothing. Come on," I urged Ava. "Here!" I responded to the nurse.

"Follow me to the back. First, we're gonna get your weight. Then you're gonna go into exam room 2," the nurse said looking at me then over to Ava.

"This is my friend Ava," I said as Ava sarcastically chuckled. Thank God she didn't say anything slick. "She's here for moral support."

"Oh okay. Hi, Ava," the nurse said as I stood on the scale.

"Oh wow! You've lost eight pounds since last week," the nurse said.

"I'm surprised it's not more than that the way I've been running to the bathroom lately. I can't seem to keep anything on my stomach."

"Well, hopefully, Dr. Lee will be able to help fix that."

Once we were done getting my weight, all three of us headed into the exam room and the nurse took my vitals.

"The doctor will be in to see you shortly."

Ava and I sat in silence while we waited for the doctor to come into the room.

"Shit I hope he hurries up. My nerves about to get the best of me. If he don't bring his ass in here soon, I'ma have to run to the bathroom."

As soon as I said that, there was a knock on the door then Doctor Lee walked in.

"Hello, Mr. Brown, and who is this lovely lady you have with you today?"

"She's my friend Ava. I brought her for moral support. I just felt like since I needed to come in to get my results, it must be bad and for that reason, I didn't want to come alone."

"Hmm, I see. Well-" the Doctor began, but I cut him off. Just from the tone of his "Well", I knew it was bad.

"Oh Jesus! I have cancer, don't I?" I all but cried.

"You don't have cancer Mr. Washington, but your HIV test came back positive."

"Say that again?" I asked as Ava looked up with her mouth hanging damn near on the floor. "What did you just say?"

"We did extensive blood work to determine what was going on with you. Your blood work came back positive for HIV."

"There must be some kind of mistake! Are you sure you didn't get my records confused with someone else's?" I asked nervously. HIV? Was he serious right now?

"I'm positive that didn't happen. The lab was very careful."

"Oh God! I'm gonna die!" I wailed.

"It's not as bad as you think Mr. Washington."

"Like hell it ain't! HIV is a death wish. Jesus, Mary, and Joseph!" I broke down.

"It's actually not the end of the world. Back when HIV first became known it was, but now there's medication that not only helps with the effects from having it, but there is even a medication on the market that hides the symptoms."

"Now why on earth would anyone want to hide the fact that they have HIV?" Ava interjected and I'm glad she asked. I was totally rendered speechless and was glad she was able to speak in my defense.

"Various reasons I suppose," Doctor Lee replied.

As Doctor Lee sat there rambling off a bunch of medical shit having to do with HIV, then handing me a pamphlet on how to live with, I zoned completely out. I could not believe that my reckless actions got me in a bind like this. The bigger question was where did I get it from!

"Do you have any question for me?" Doctor Lee asked at the conclusion of my appointment.

"Nope, I think I have heard just about enough," I replied then took the several pieces of paper, which were prescriptions that I needed to take to the pharmacy to have filled.

As if being told that I had HIV wasn't enough, as soon as the doctor left and shut the door, Ava slapped me so hard I fell off the exam table.

"You motherfucker you! You betta hope and pray I don't have that shit! Find your own damn way home!"

Ava walked out, leaving me alone in the exam room and all I could do was break down and cry. My life as I once knew it was now officially over and I couldn't blame not a soul but myself.

Ava

When the doctor told Shane that he had HIV, I thought I was going to have a legit heart attack right where I was sitting. I couldn't believe that shit. I felt bad for Shane and all, but

I felt even worse for myself. Knowing that he and Justin were fucking around I couldn't help but to panic. When I slapped his ass off the exam table, he was lucky I didn't knock the shit out of him too. I was livid to say the least. I knew that there was no chance in hell I was going to carry his ass back home after finding that shit out.

He got himself in that position, so it was going to be on him to figure out the rest. I didn't feel bad at all for leaving his ass right where he was. When I made it to my car, I immediately looked up my doctor's number and called the office. Not only was I angry, but I was embarrassed to have to call my doctor and admit that my husband had cheated on me and possibly exposed me to HIV.

His office accommodated me and let me come in right away to get a blood test. You would have sworn I was being chased by how fast I jetted out of the parking lot at Shane's doctor's office then headed to mine. I didn't even care that I was speeding. I felt like if the police pulled up behind me, and pulled me over, I was ready to tell them that it was a matter of life and death.

I was so angry that I didn't know what to think or who to call. I figured this was something that I was going to have to keep to myself until I found out what the results were.

"About how long is it going to take for me to get the results?" I asked Julie, the nurse that worked at my doctor's office.

"Oh, about twenty minutes for the rapid test. We also send the blood work whether it's positive or negative just to be sure."

"Twenty minutes! Wow!"

"Yeah, technology and medicine are no joke nowadays."

"Tell me about it."

"I'll be back shortly," Julie said then left me alone in the room to myself.

If that test came back positive, I was gonna have to prepare myself to live out the rest of my life in jail for the murders of Shane and Justin. About 30 minutes later, there was a knock on the door then Julie walked in along with my doctor.

"Welp, the rapid test came back negative. However, just to be sure we will still send your blood work to the lab."

"Oh, thank God. What are the chances of it coming back positive?"

"It's really hard to say. With medicine you just never know. I will say this, usually if the rapid test is negative the blood work will be also. But you just never know. Everyone is different, which is why we still send the blood work out to the lab."

"I can't believe this!"

"I'm so sorry you are going through this. I will say this though. If your blood work comes back positive, it's not the end of the world. There are several different types of medication that will mask the symptoms. But we will hold off on having that conversation until we get your lab results. For now, practice safe sex and you should be hearing back from our office in a few days. If it will help, I'll even make the lab work stat, so it won't take as long as usual."

"I would love that! Thanks so much for squeezing me into the schedule on such short notice. I just can't believe that all of this is happening to me."

"You're most welcome. Here's the printout of the rapid results in case you need them for your records. If you have any questions, don't hesitate to give our office a call."

Leaving out of the doctor's office, I felt a little at ease. I knew that I was going to still be worried until I heard back from them about my lab results.

Chapter Thirteen

Ava

Two Weeks Later

I was excited about today because I was going to look at a townhouse for rent that was on the same block as my sister's house. Over the past two weeks, I was able to move out the rest of my belongings with the help of not just my sister but Kevin as well. I didn't have very much stuff to move out, but it was quite a bit. So much so that I was going to have to rent a public storage bin. Kevin was gracious enough to not only help us move, because Lord only knew we definitely needed the manpower, but he allowed for me to store my things in his basement. It was a few furniture pieces, several boxes of clothes, home decor and kitchen appliances.

Hopefully, I would not only like the townhouse that I was going to look at, but I'd be able to sign a lease today as well. As I was getting dressed, I got a phone call from an unknown number. I wasn't going to answer it at first, but when I took a closer look the number kind of looked familiar.

"Hello," I answered, hoping it wasn't a solicitor because I loathed those types of phones calls.

"Hello, my name is Brandon, the head nurse at the trauma center at Advocate Hospital. May I speak with Ava Miller please?"

Holy shit! What the hell was the hospital calling me for? "This is Ava, what is this call pertaining to?"

I instantly got weak because I hoped that it wasn't about my HIV blood work. My lab results had come in a week ago and I was in the clear. For the hospital to be calling me now, I hoped that they hadn't made a mistake and that they weren't calling to tell me that my results were positive and not negative.

"I'm calling you because you are listed in our system as the next of kin for Justin Miller."

When he said Justin's name I was shocked. I hadn't talked to him since I caught his ass. I had his number on block and left it that way ever since. As far as the divorce was concerned, my lawyer was the one initiating all communication with him, so to hear his name and to know he was in the hospital had me a bit concerned.

"Is everything okay?"

"Well, not quite. He was involved in an accident at his job and has been admitted. We need you to come to the hospital as soon as possible please."

"What kind of accident? Is he going to be okay?"

"Rather than discuss this over the phone, for the patient's privacy it would be best if you come into the hospital and we sit face to face."

"Okay, I'm on my way."

Hanging up with the hospital, I called out to Dawn.

"Dawn! Dawn! I'll be right back. Justin's been in some kind of accident and the hospital just called asking me to come in."

"What happened na?" Dawn asked speed walking into the den where I was sitting. "Why they calling you? Are you really going to go check for ass after everything that happened?"

"Not now Dawn. At the end of the day, he is still my husband. Our divorce isn't quite final because he hasn't signed the papers yet. So yes, to answer your question I'm going to see what's going on."

"Hold up, I'll ride with."

"As long as you won't be with the shits, fine. But if not, I think it's best if you stay here and I'll call you and keep you posted."

"Nonsense! I'm coming. You act like I don't know how to conduct myself."

"It is questionable."

"Oh hush, I'll be right back. Just let me go get my shoes," Dawn huffed then took off to go get her stuff.

She was taking longer than my patience could handle. I didn't realize it was going to take forever for her to go put on some shoes.

"I'll be in the car!" I hollered out headed to my car.

Ten minutes later, Dawn joined me then we headed for the hospital.

"Did they say what happened?"

"No, all the nurse said was that he was in an accident while at work. He didn't want to give me any more information over the phone."

"Oh, this sounds bad."

"I swear you always think so negatively," I said.

"I do not! I'm just being realistic!" Dawn said.

We rode the rest of the way in silence as it only took me ten minutes to get to the hospital. I chose to valet park because I didn't feel like walking the long distance from the parking lot to the entrance. Making it inside, we stopped at the front desk that was in the lobby and asked for Justin's room number. The lady behind the desk told us which elevator to take and we set in tow to find out what was going on with Justin.

"Hello, my name is Ava Miller. I got a call from a nurse about Justin Miller."

"Oh yes, hello Mrs. Miller-"

"You can call me Ava," I interrupted.

"Nice to meet you Ava. Thanks for coming."

"No problem. This is my sister Dawn. What's going on with Justin?"

"Let's go to a room so that I can explain, but first I need you to sign these HIPPA forms."

After signing the forms, Dawn and I followed the nurse to an empty patient room.

"Mr. Miller was at the scene of a fire and had a pretty bad fall this morning. He broke his hip and suffered smoke inhalation pretty badly. He is scheduled for surgery today. We are just waiting for the on-call surgeon to get here."

"Ha, that's all. I thought his ass-" Dawn started but I stopped her.

"Not now Dawn!"

The nurse looked from me to her then led us to Justin's room.

"He is in quite a bit of pain, overall. But he is alert and anxiously waiting to be taken in for surgery."

When I walked into Justin's room, his eyes lit up and it looked like he was going to cry. Tate was in the room with him and when he saw Dawn, it looked like he had seen a ghost. I'm guessing he felt a little uncomfortable being in her presence after things didn't work out between them.

"Ava baby, you came! I didn't think you would come."

"I only came because it sounded a lot more serious over the phone. I didn't think I had a choice to come or not. Hello Tate," I said turning my attention to his friend.

"Hey Ava," Tate responded giving me a hug, "Hello Dawn, nice to see you."

"Hey Tate," Dawn responded then rolled her eyes at Justin.

Neither Justin nor Dawn spoke to each other and I was cool with that.

"Thanks for coming. They saying that I have to have hip surgery. My recovery is going to be hell. I'm so happy you're here with me."

"I only came because I thought it was more serious than what it actually is." I wasn't standing here trying to fake anything for his ass. Hip surgery! They didn't even need to call me at all.

"What do you mean more serious?! A broken hip isn't serious to you?"

"Not exactly. It wasn't serious enough for me to come down here! Once the surgery is over, in time you'll recover," I responded. "Seeing as how this isn't anything major, I'm gonna go ahead and leave."

"Wait! What do you mean you're leaving?! You just got here."

"Justin we are no longer together. I'm not trying to give the wrong impression by being here."

"Wow! Really Ava?! I just told you that my recovery is going to be hell. I need you to be here. I can't ask Tate to stay because he has work."

"So do I!"

"Really?! You gone kick me like this when I'm already down bad?" Justin asked in a sad voice. He had to be shitting me if he thought I was going to feel sorry for his ass!

"Call Shane! I'm sure he's biting at the bits to come help you."

"Wow!" Justin said as if he was shocked.

"Speaking of Shane, where is he?" I asked being sarcastic.

"See, now you're just being downright nasty!" Justin spat.

"Nasty as in catching the two of you together nasty?!" I sneered. "Speaking of Shane, have you talked to him lately?"

"No, after that day, I haven't said nothing else to his ass. I'm sorry Ava baby, please you have to know that I'm sorry."

"Oh, sorry is not the right word! You're more like pathetic! You might want to call your boy up. He may have some important information for you."

I had already told my sister about the whole HIV thing once my blood work came back from the lab negative. She was standing there soaking this all up. Judging from the look on her face, she was enjoying every minute of me and Justin's back and forth banter.

"What information could he possibly have for me?" Justin asked.

Well, I wasn't trying to be the bearer of bad news, but aye... as long as I was here!

"He tested positive for HIV, fool! I hope you used protection because if not you might want to get yourself checked out while you're here."

Tate jumped up from the chair he was sitting in with a look a terror on his face.

"You son of a bitch! I trusted you, bro!" Tate shouted pointing his finger at Justin.

Justin just sat there with his mouth hung open and his eyes bucked.

"I can't believe this shit! How could you be so careless?" Tate continued to fuss.

"Hold the hell up! Was you fucking this nigga too?" Dawn shouted jumping up and down. "I knew it! I knew something was off with Tate's ass too! Aww hell nah Justin, who else's booty you been diggin' in?" Dawn asked as she busted out laughing and Tate ran out of the room.

"Now wait one minute! What the hell are you talking about Ava? You shouldn't be here if you just came to get me upset. I'm the patient here and that's some bullshit for you to prance up in here talking bullshit."

"You think so huh? Hold on right quick," I responded, pulling my cellphone out of my purse and calling Shane's number then putting the phone on speaker. The phone rang all of two times before Shane answered.

"Ava," Shane sang into the phone. "I'm surprised to be hearing from you."

"Why is that?" I asked.

"When you stormed out of the doctor's office that day, I didn't think that I would ever hear from you again," Shane said.

"Yeah, well I didn't think I would ever be calling you again. I just wanted you to know that I went and got tested," I informed him.

"Please tell me that you didn't catch HIV! Oh God, I'm so sorry Ava!" Shane cried out.

"Oh no, hunny!" I responded sarcastically. "My test came back negative, but I was just wondering, did you ever tell Justin about your positive HIV status?" I asked as I starred Justin in the eyes.

"I've called him a few times to let him know he should get tested, but he has been avoiding me," Shane said sadly.

"Okay then, well you just told him now because he just heard every word you said. I got you on speaker," I responded then hung up the phone.

Walking up to the side of Justin's bed as he laid there with the look of horror in his eyes, I smacked him as hard as I could across his face.

Turning around to leave, Tate was standing there glaring at Justin while Dawn was digging in her purse. I was hoping that she wasn't going to pull out a weapon because I didn't want to catch a charge for abusing a patient. Pulling out a familiar looking paper, she handed them to Justin.

"Oh, and by the way, sign these divorce papers before we leave before I have to whip your ass again up in this bitch!" Dawn spat as I looked at her like she was crazy.

No wonder it took her forever to get her shoes back at the house. She was in my room looking through my shit for my divorce papers.

I couldn't even be mad at her though. I needed those papers signed like yesterday. Dawn handed Justin a pen so that he could sign the papers, then I snatched them off of the bedside table she placed them on and left.

It felt good to get all of that off my chest. The look on Justin's face would be one that I would never forget. Leaving the hospital that day, I never felt better. I felt free, vindicated and finally happy.

Made in the USA
Columbia, SC
10 June 2020